Sara Sigourney Rice, Mary A Niemeyer

Light in Darkness

Autobiography of Mary A. Niemeyer

Sara Sigourney Rice, Mary A Niemeyer

Light in Darkness
Autobiography of Mary A. Niemeyer

ISBN/EAN: 9783337028640

Printed in Europe, USA, Canada, Australia, Japan

Cover: Foto ©Raphael Reischuk / pixelio.de

More available books at **www.hansebooks.com**

LIGHT IN DARKNESS.

AUTOBIOGRAPHY

OF

MARY A. NIEMEYER.

———•◆•———

"While others gaze on Nature's face,
The verdant vale, the mountains, woods and streams,
Or with delight ineffable survey
The Sun, bright image of this parent God;
Whilst others view Heaven's all-involving arch,
Bright with unnumber'd worlds, and lost in joy,
Fair order and utility behold.
To me those fair vicissitudes are lost,
And grace and beauty blotted from my view."
— DR. THOMAS BLACKLOCK.

———•◆•———

REVISED

BY

SARA S. RICE.

———•◆•———

PHILADELPHIA:
PRINTED BY J. B. LIPPINCOTT & CO.
1878.

PREFACE.

GENTLE READER: It is not supposed you have opened
this book to read, expecting to find rare intellectual
pleasure, or the gratification of any sense of thrilling
romance. Were this so, its lids should at once be closed,
and its very name forgotten. It is a life-history, not
startling in any degree, but its object has been to show,
though He afflict, how good God is. Truly there has
been light in darkness all the way along. We have hoped
to serve His cause in the lessons drawn even from the
small events of life, and we trust the modest messenger
may bear some note of cheer to hearts that have known
earthly sorrow, and enliven, perhaps, for an evening fireside hour, the gathered family group.

Light in Darkness.

AUTOBIOGRAPHY OF MARY A. NIEMEYER.

---•◦•---

CHAPTER I.

"There is a land of every land the pride,
Beloved by Heaven o'er all the world beside."
Montgomery.

"Breathes there a man with soul so dead,
Who never to himself hath said,
This is my own, my native land!"
Scott.

In the village of Deisel, about twenty-four miles from the city of Cassel, Germany, the subject of this biography was born. Here her eyes first greeted the light of day; first saw Nature robed in her varied mantles, green in the early Springtime, sun-tinged and yellow in the strong Summer season; brown, red and sere in the sombre Autumn; and snow-white when Winter had folded the blossoms of flower and fruit away in his bosom, there to sleep till awakened to life and vigor again by the returning Spring.

A brief description of this quiet village, nestled as it is beneath the wing of the better known and farther famed city of Cassel, may not be uninteresting. It is inhabited principally by farmers, its population numbering between two and three thousand people. While the pursuits are mostly agricultural, as in all other villages, various occupations afford a livelihood to the residents.

The streets are regularly laid out, and are kept neat and clean. The dwellings are large and comfortable, with gardens and orchards attached. The Reformed is the prevailing religious belief. There is but one Church in the place; this is very large and built in Gothic style. It is noted for its chime of bells, well known to the villagers, and loved by them for their sweetly falling cadences or swelling notes, pealing forth on the Sabbath morning air, calling them to worship within the sacred temple.

The organ, with the characteristic love of good music, peculiar to the Germans as a nation, is of course superior in volume and quality of tone, capable, as a consequence, of producing both strength and delicacy of expression. The Germans revel in music, either sacred or otherwise, and Sabbath or week days, it constitutes a part of their enjoyment.

The services are always well attended. The children of the village day school, both boys and girls, occupy the galleries, near the organ, and their sweet voices blend in rich and complete harmony with the fuller and deeper tones of the instrument, making a glad gush of melody, inspiring to both heart and brain of the oldest worshipper, and bringing back mayhap in full tide a rush of happy memories of times, when voices now cracked and shrill, were equally clear and ringing.

The Church is open for service twice every Sabbath, morning and afternoon. Very neat and trim the villagers look, as in their best attire they wend their way to the House of God. They remember the command, "Six days shalt thou labor and do all thy work: but the seventh day is the Sabbath of the Lord thy God: in it thou shalt not do any work." They are devout in their bearing, and hallow this day of days as one of God's greatest blessings to man.

There is also a large and well-arranged
school house in the village. The school is
divided into two departments: first, the primary, where the children remain three years,
and are instructed in the rudiments of education. Then follows a higher department,
where the full course is five years. Here a
finished and even elegant education may be
obtained, and the student may graduate with
justly earned honors. The industrious become
highly creditable in their scholastic attainments, as they have every facility afforded
them. Their graduation, however, renders
incumbent upon them early confirmation to
the Reformed Church, catechetical instruction
having been part of their education. The
children are trained in the religious views of
their parents, and are not so likely to wander
off and become members of other denominations as soon as they arrive at maturity.
Ties are more closely knit if a whole family
worship in one way. Divided religious sentiment is perhaps more potent than any other
influence in separating the interests and affections of a home circle. It is a rock, flower
crowned it may be, still one that has wrecked
many a household bark.

The country surrounding the village is exceedingly beautiful. A stretch of landscape most pleasing to the beholder and refreshing to the senses, is spread out, with lavish beauty decked. The public roads leading to this open land are very wide. They are also well shaded by fine trees planted in rows on each side of the road. Thus avenues are formed, in which it is delightful to stroll during the warm Summer weather.

Travel is mostly on foot. In order to afford comfort and rest to the pedestrian, neat and inviting arbors are stationed all along the way, at the distance of about a mile apart. Thus the fatigue of a long walk is obviated; and what might otherwise be attended with discomfort, is made pleasurable and inviting. The healthful exercise of walking is much indulged in, and doubtless has its influence in preventing any dyspeptic tendency among the people. With these arbors in which to rest if weary, one cannot wonder at this habit of the villagers. They are indeed charming spots, where the traveller may be screened from the heat of the noonday sun. Or children in their gambols and heyday play, may find in them refuge from the sudden storm, threatening dis-

may, were it not for these wayside shelterers.
But as they know these safe retreats are near
at hand, they fearlessly anticipate the storm,
ready to escape to their refuge at the first vivid
flash of the lightning in zigzag lines athwart
the sky; or at the low muttered roll of the
thunder's distant voice.

The country is beautifully diversified with
hills and valleys, green fields and meadows,
and one can but admire the panorama of
beauty spread out before them. Not least
among the natural attractions, are the hedges
of various kinds enclosing the fields. These
bloom the greater part of the year forming bright borders of many hues, and giving the whole country a fresh and lovely
appearance.

The village is a busy, bustling place. Activity and diligence are everywhere apparent.
No signs of sloth and indolence are visible.
Each morning the farmer may be seen driving
his cattle through the streets, and bearing his
farming implements and other necessary uten-
sils out to the fields, that are to be tilled, or
sown, or reaped. With glad face and hopeful
heart he goes forth, for he knows labor will bring
its own reward. The fields are spread before

him, and wait but his diligent hand " to laugh
in harvest." Other workmen, too, may be
seen engaged in their various occupations, but
all equally evidencing good will and strong
purpose, that must overcome every obstacle,
and in the end secure solid advantage.

This is no fancy sketch. This modest little
village is all I have pictured it—a thriving,
prosperous place—and the sturdy enterprise of
its people, of course, makes it what it is. God
gives man his opportunity, he must use it if he
would not have his life a failure. He must
toil, " must earn his bread by the sweat of his
brow," or sink to the level of the brute that
browses on the plain ; or lower still, to that of
the creature that needs not the soft grass for a
couch, but takes a bed whose miry consistence
suits best his grovelling nature. Labor is a
God-like principle. It lifts man nearer his
first and lost estate. It makes a second Eden
of the earth in which we live. It always
brings with it sweet recompense, slumber to
the weary, hope to the downcast, and every
blessing the largest desire could demand. If
we have nobly striven in our sphere, whatever
it may be, we may surely expect " after life's
fitful fever," when death heaves in view,

> "To approach the grave
> Like one who wraps the drapery of his couch
> About him, and lies down to pleasant dreams."

With its people occupied in various ways, some off in the fields, others in their homes, Deisel during the day presents a deserted appearance. The streets are quiet, the houses closed, even the children are not heard. But when evening comes on, and the farmers return from the fields, the workmen from their shops, the wives and mothers have finished their daily domestic employments, and the children are out of school, the scene is a most lively one. The streets are cheerful, doors and windows are open, and the merry sound of happy voices falls on the ear, and the village seems as "for a feast arrayed."

The people are lively and fond of music. They spend their evenings in social gatherings. Singing is one of their chief enjoyments. They, however, have other amusements, for they are a pleasure-loving people, and games of various kinds are participated in by both old and young. This is a delightful way to close the day. All care is forgotten in the evening, and mirth and jollity reign supreme.

The climate is salubrious and healthful.

This, added to their thrifty, prudent habits, makes the inhabitants sturdy and vigorous. You seldom meet a man, woman or child, whose cheek is not mantled with the rosy blush of health. There is generally no resident physician in the place, for the simple and very satisfactory reason, his services are too seldom required to afford one even a moderate amount of occupation, and, of course, no sufficient compensation could be secured to ensure a livelihood. Hence, Dame Nature is her children's almoner of healing draughts, and her cures are oftener attained than are those of some more modern modes of treatment. She, at least, is not a quack, and suggests no astonishing remedy as panacea for all the woes of humankind. She is a physician, good and true, who, her laws observed, gives in exchange health and long life. But do her laws violence, throw aside her simple teachings for those higher sounding in their unintelligible terms, and naught but woe and sore distress will follow; a life made up of ills, for which there is no redress this side the grave.

In Deisel the women are famous for their industry. They are not idle even in their hours of relaxation; but generally are like good old John Gilpin's wife—

> " Who, though on pleasure she was bent,
> She had a frugal mind."

You see them constantly with knitting in their hands, diligently plying the swiftly flying needles, till the well-knit hose, the tidy neck comforter, or the warm winter hood, is wrought. In their walks, too, it is no uncommon thing to see them thus employed, destroying perhaps to some extent the teaching of the old and long accepted maxim, " One cannot do well any two things at a time."

CHAPTER II.

"Why is the hearse with 'scutcheons blazoned round,
And with nodding plumes of ostrich crowned?
                                        Gay's Trivia.

"I do love these ancient ruins:
We never tread upon them, but we set
Our foot upon some rev'rend history.
                            Webster's Duchess of Malfy.

"Heigh ho! daisies and buttercups,
Fair yellow daffodils, stately and tall—
A sunshiny world full of laughter and leisure,
And fresh hearts unconscious of sorrow and thrall."
                                        Jean Ingelow.

"The fading many-colored woods,
Shade deep'ning over shade, the country round
Imbrown."
                                        Jas. Thomson.

The customs of Deisel are, in some respects,
peculiar to itself, and in a degree individualize
the otherwise not remarkable place. Funerals
have here some features not elsewhere observed.
The authorities require the corpse to be retained
in the house three days before burial. This is
to determine beyònd a doubt if life is really

extinct, and to give the apparently lifeless form every possible chance of revivification. The people have a superstitious horror of burying a friend alive, and take every precaution to prevent so sad a catastrophe. If the pulse be surely still in death, if every means have failed to restore animation, they further proceed to prepare the remains for interment. The body is placed in a coffin; if the deceased were less than twenty-five years of age, the coffin is decorated with plumes, ribbons and flowers; if over twenty-five years, it is draped with heavy black cloth, on which are inscribed verses of Scripture, in gilt letters, the sentiment appropriate to the event commemorated.

Singing funerals are those occasions, where plaintive music depicts the virtues of the dead and the sorrow of the living. These are observed only in memory of grown persons. The teachers and scholars of the village school are well trained in vocal music. They assemble at the house where the funeral is to take place, and the singing obsequies are conducted entirely by them. Several hymns, dirge-like and sad, are sung at the house; after which the minister offers a prayer. Then the musicians, friends and mourners, form a procession, and walk, carrying the remains, to the cemetery. The teachers and scholars lead, singing as they go a low, sweet melody, in memory of the dead. Behind them are six men, the pall-bearers. They bear on their shoulders the coffin. Next, the relatives and friends of the deceased, clad in mourning, and bewailing the loss of their loved one, move slowly forward.

The burial ground is about a quarter of a mile from the village. When it is reached the body is lowered into the grave. All the while the music has continued. The bells have been tolling, and the scene is altogether a most impressive one. The ceremony of interment over, the company wend their way to the church. There a sermon is delivered. The virtues of the departed are recounted, and a lesson is drawn for the living.

Once more all meet at the house where the funeral took place. This time they assemble to partake of a repast prepared for the occasion. Thus it is, life with death is blended. We mourn and weep, but ere long forget the pall and shroud and last adieu. We soon recall but dimly amid the bustle of the world's ongoing, the friend we have lost. This may be well. It would not be best for us to brood too

long or deeply over our sorrow. We owe
duties to the living and must put our grief
aside, that we may be able to fufil them.
There is comfort for hearts that are bowed
down, in the thought that, although there is a
time for sighing, there cometh also a season for
rejoicing.   To-night may be dark, to-mor-
row, radiant with light, so checkered is our
way.

Another custom peculiar to Deisel is the
dedication of the dwellings.   When a new
house is finished, the villagers collect, form a
procession, and pass through the streets, headed
by two young men carrying a bush. This bush
is trimmed with wreaths, boquets and ribbons.
Six young girls follow dressed in gay colors,
crowned with flowers, and holding boquets in
their hands. Following these again are the
men, women and children of the village, all
singing songs suitable to the occasion. When
the house is reached, the bush is placed upon
the roof and securely fastened there. This is
a fanciful house crowning, it is true, but is
symbolic in its usage. Songs and speeches are
in order, and a festive time is made of it. A
dinner follows, and every delicacy tempts the
palate. The idea of thus introducing into a

new dwelling mirth and gladness, is surely an
excellent one. Were such genii more frequently to preside in our homes, clouds would
not settle on the domestic horizon, but would
drift away, leaving no trace behind them.
There is a good and kindly sentiment in the
custom, and a dash of poetry beside.

When passing through the forests in this
part of Germany, one can but observe the
unusual appearance of the soil. It has every
indication of having been, at some remote
period, cultivated. The wanderer will also
meet with relics of a bygone time in the ruins
of ancient castles; their demolished walls and
dilapidated towers reminding only of a glory
past, and causing the thoughtful to pause and
ponder on the mutability of all mere earthly
greatness, how surely it must crumble into
waste and nothingness.

There are also scattered ruins of towns,
which probably had been destroyed by war
hundreds of years ago, and which are now only
to be recognized in these vestiges of their former
selves. This is the acme of all human history,
to rise, flourish for a day, then to pass away,
giving place to another busy, bustling scene of
action, and leaving to others the parts in life's

drama, some may have vainly fancied they could best perform. It is well we are not left to our own discretion as to our ability to do, or our worthiness to be considered; for were we so left, we should make grave errors. It is therefore wisest that all our changes are chosen for us.

There comes welling up from my heart a full tide of tender, cherished memories, as I thus recall the characteristics of my childhood's home, and I can but linger among these scenes of my youth. To sketch them in all their varied beauty, would be a task quite beyond my feeble pen; but if words, warm from a loving heart, can fitly portray these visions of a day that is fled, I shall at least secure kindly sympathy from those who may with me visit the land that gave me birth, and the home where first I learned to lisp a mother's name. Gentle reader, you and I are children again. We will bask in the sunshine together, listen to the carol of the summer birds, see mirrored in the crystal brook our laughing eyes and health crowned cheeks; for not then had my sky been darkened, not even a misty cloud had shown itself; I looked upon Nature and saw her loveliness, with no thought of a future with-

out a ray from sun or moon or star, to illumine
it. I little thought then that ere many years
had fled, the sight of all external objects would
be lost to me. But we will leave the shadows
for the present, and luxuriate in the bright and
beautiful.

In the village of Deisel the season of Spring
seemed especially delightful. Children might
be seen constantly in merry groups, gathering
flowers, the spontaneous product of the soil;
for verily the hills, meadows, dales, hedges and
banks of streamlets, were covered with every
variety of floral growth. Beautiful blossoms
of all forms and colors, some appearing so
choice and delicate, one would suppose they
needed the most careful culture, sprang unbid-
den from the earth. They looked with tender
eyes, soft and blue, or with blushes deeper than
of crimson dye, from verdant beds up into our
faces, with a greeting in their own, and breathed
on the welcoming air a fragrance entrancing to
the senses.

I often fancy even now, though years have
passed since these scenes were spread before
me, that I am again with my little companions,
plucking these beautiful flowers, filling our
aprons with them, tossing some aloft, to see

3

them scatter their delicate petals and fall to the earth, shorn of their loveliness. Then we are trying to see if butter is loved, by placing the saucy buttercup under the chin, or having a wild hunt for a lady's slipper, seeking the modest daisy, wherewith to make a chain to entrap some wanderer from elf-land; running about to search for a desolate bachelor's button, or perhaps hiding away a Sweet William, to see if the fairies would send a prince by that name to woo some fair Cinderella, with her pumpkin coach and slipper of glass.

Thus we revelled among the flowers till Autumn, with its nuts and berries, came. Then we sped to the woods and loaded ourselves with the toothsome things, and brought them home as trophies to our mothers, who carefully stowed them away for Winter's fireside enjoyment.

During the seasons of Spring, Summer, and ofttimes far into the Autumn, the public pleasure gardens, situated a short distance from the village, are favorite resorts for the people. They are laid out in walks, with flower beds and vine-covered arbors scattered here and there. The amusements are music and dancing. These are participated in by persons of all ages, and

for a few hours of each evening everybody is
seeking recreation. Refreshment can be had
at a small cost, which aids in making these
gardens almost social in their character.

The seasons over admitting outdoor pleasures, and the winter, with its frosts and chilling
winds, making the fireside attractive, the young
men and women gather at each other's houses.
They bring their spinning wheels with them,
for flax is one of the principal products of this
part of Germany. The evening hours are
spent in chat and song, intermingled with the
steady whirring of the busy wheel. Children
at the age of nine and ten years can spin as
well as some grown persons. Time flies swiftly
and agreeably, mirth and industry filling the
hours. Thrift is made attractive, and becomes
characteristic of the people. And often too at
such times a certain sly little god, with bow
and arrow ready to command, forms one of the
number in these assemblies, and other threads
are spun than those that wind out in lengthen-
ing line from the steadily turning wheel.
Heart and foot and hand keep time until a
web of life is formed, and the sly god, with
emptied quiver, laughs at the mischief he has
done.

CHAPTER III.

"Life is from Thee, blessed Father,
From Thee our breathing spirits;
And Thou dost give to all that live
The bliss that each inherits."

R. Ware, Jr.

"Thou art the victor, Death!
Thou comest, and where is that which spoke
From the depths of the eye, when the bright soul woke?
Gone with the flitting breath!

Felicia Hemans.

My parents and grandparents were born in Deisel. My parents were companions at school. At the age of fourteen they were confirmed at the same altar. When eighteen years old, my father went to the military school. He remained there five years as student, and a year and a half as officer. He would have remained longer, but being the eldest son, was needed at home to assist his father, who was engaged in farming, and who was also carrying on extensively the boot and shoe business.

Upon his return, the early friendship, which had existed between my father and mother when children, was renewed. The feeling ripened into a strong attachment, and they were married in a short time.

My mother was the youngest child of her parents; so, according to the usage of the country, my father went to reside at her home. The old homestead was given up to them, my grand parents living with them. Shortly after her marriage, my mother's father died, full of years, and ripe for the tomb. A life well spent brought with its close no unavailing regrets.

I have frequently heard my mother speak of his death as the calmest she had ever witnessed. During the day on which he died, he was more composed than usual. With perfect resignation he told his family he should not see the dawn of another day. When they tried to persuade him this impression was only a fancy, he insisted that they would find he was correct, and that ere the day had passed he should be no more.

He besought all his family to be faithful to their God; to serve Him diligently; to lead noble, honorable lives, doing all the good within their power while in the world, that when death should come, they could sink peacefully to rest, with no remorse to make bitter their last hours. He urged those near and dear to

him on earth to meet him in heaven. He then
in failing accents, murmured the touching lines:

"Earthly home, adieu, adieu,
Earthly friends, farewell to you
Softly breathe your last good-bye,
Jesus calls me, let me die."

The cold sweat of death had settled on his
brow, his voice grew inarticulate, and the
spirit fled to the God who gave it.

A few months later my grandmother died.
She missed the strong arm she had leaned
upon, and followed in a little while her husband. Death did not sunder them long. God
was very good, and took her to Himself. Earth
had no charms for her, separated from him by
whose side she had stood in sunshine and storm
for many years. She rejoiced as she neared
the swelling tide of Jordan's waves, and with
a bright smile on her face she passed away. It
seemed as though she had had a greeting from
the heavenly land, ere with folded hands she
fell asleep never to waken more. These were
cherished memories with my mother, and she
often told us of the last days of our grandparents. It was her earnest desire so to end
her life, calmly, peacefully, yet full of a blissful
hope beyond the grave.

At the time of these occurrences I was an infant of fifteen months. My grandparents were dotingly fond of me. My grandmother watched over me with unceasing care. I was very delicate, and she feared the frail babe might let go her slender hold on life. Over and over again have these things been told me, till I have almost thought I myself knew them to be facts.

My father's mother died in middle life, and in a few years my grandfather married again. The lady who became his second wife had been the belle of the village. She was very attractive in personal appearance. She was devoted to fashion and gaiety. Her heart seemed wholly given up to worldly pleasure. Her tastes were extravagant, and she indulged them to the utmost. My grandfather married this lady after an acquaintance of six months. He lost sight of the disparity between their modes of living, and did not appear to be aware of her frivolity of character. His children regretted the step he had taken. They concluded to leave home. My father was the eldest of seven children, and had been some time married. My grandfather's second marriage did not affect his domestic happiness, as he was not living with his father. But the other children felt keenly the change in their home.

After a few weeks' wedding tour, the newly married couple returned to find themselves the sole occupants of the house. Grandfather had not expected this; but his children refused to call his wife mother; nor would they endure to see her take their mother's place. They requested that some provision by which they could make a livelihood, should be made for them. They had resolved to seek a home elsewhere. The old homestead had now no charm for them. Its light had fled; the steady light of maternal love had gone out, not to be rekindled. Their father acceded to their wishes. Five of the family settled in the neighboring towns. One sailed for America, to try the experiences of a new country. My father only remained in the village.

Thus a family was scattered, and those fondly attached were separated, never again to form an unbroken household. The providence was inscrutable. Life's cup may be filled to the brim with sweets, yet contain one bitter drop. Our lots may have much of joy in them, but there will lurk in each some sorrow. It is the world's great lesson, which all humanity must learn. To us remains only resignation. We must unmurmuringly submit to circumstances and dispensations beyond our control. Sooner or later all must accept this truth, for we hold not the issues of a single moment. To us life is mystery, but there is One who knoweth every hidden thing, and in His own good time He will reveal.

My father and mother were very comfortably situated. Our family group was a happy one. The merry ring of childish laughter dispelled all gloom. My mother was cheerful and contented. She strove to instil into our young minds lessons of truth, obedience, and love. She guided our feeble, tottering footsteps, with all a mother's watchfulness. After the toil of the day was over, and father came home, we had a joyous time. Care was forgotten, and he became a child again, and played every sort of game with his little ones. All day we longed for the evening to come, that we might enjoy these sports.

There probably is not to be found the man or woman who does not look back upon the days of childhood with all the admiration and fond romance one has for pictures drawn from fairy land. The heart must become sere indeed, that does not glow at the remembrance of the sweet voice of some prattling sister, or bounding step of a light-hearted, fun-loving brother, whose mischievous pranks may have even annoyed our girlish sense of propriety.

The house in which I was born was pleasantly located. Attached to it was a large vegetable and flower garden, also a fine orchard of various fruit trees. My grandfather had owned the property many years. He had inherited it from his father. Upon my mother's marriage, he had removed the old house and erected a new one. This was large and well-arranged, with barn and stable in the rear. It was built of stone and wood. We occupied this homestead until father decided to emigrate to America. Mother then sold it to her nephew, Henry Koester. She was anxious for the property to remain in the Schildtknecht family, as it had been owned by them for nearly a century.

My father's family had always resided very near my mother's home. The two families had been on the most intimate terms until the time of my grandfather Niemeyer's second marriage. This circumstance had produced an unfortunate estrangement. Still, as it appeared to have resulted agreeably for grandfather, his children were becoming somewhat reconciled to it. Mrs. Niemeyer had laid aside many of her excesses, was less extravagant, and showed a desire to conform to her husband's wishes and more quiet mode of life. This tended greatly to ameliorate the strong feeling of opposition to the marriage which had at first existed.

The Easter and Christmas seasons are with the Germans occasions of peculiar significance. They are celebrated, perhaps, with more form than in any other country. Thursday before Good Friday, is a joyful day to the young folks of Deisel.

An old and wealthy citizen, who was known to be especially fond of children, but who was very eccentric, had, a great number of years before my story begins, at his death left a legacy to the children of the village. This was to be used to give them a treat on the day named. The custom was one in which all took great pleasure. All the little boys and girls between infancy and fourteen years of age, dressed in their best attire, proceeded to the Churchyard. Here a table was spread with everything that was tempting to the eye

and palate. The afternoon was appropriated
to the enjoyment of this repast. Never will
any who partook of the good things so gener-
ously provided for them, forget the pleasures
of these festival days. The memory of the
kind donor who had made happy so many
childish hearts, was always touchingly referred
to, and a thought of gratitude was cherished
by even the tiniest little one present.

At Easter great preparations are made for
the students who are to be confirmed. The
outfit for the occasion is white. It is presented
to the candidates by their god-parents. The
Churches at this season are beautifully decked
with evergreens and flowers; and the ceremony
of confirmation is very solemn and imposing.
My parents had the pleasure of seeing two of
their children confirmed before leaving their
native land.

On Easter Monday the young people hold a
pic-nic a short distance from the village. The
principal feature of the day is the great variety
of Easter-eggs. These are beautifully colored,
and the children find great amusement in
"picking" them. This is in observance of an
old custom handed down from the remote past.
Easter-fires, Easter-eggs, and many other cus-

toms and superstitions, have all their origin
from the ancient heathen feast, which, as the
celebration of the resurrection of Nature, was
very appropriately succeeded by the festival
which commemorates the resurrection of Christ.
But the children do not moralize upon the
meaning of the breaking of the egg to let fly
the hidden bird, symbol as it is of the opening
grave that the buried Christ might rise. They
have yet to learn that even in their pastimes is
often deeper significance than they had ever
thought.

With the rites of the joyous Christmas
season the village children are more familiar.
Their voices chorus jubilantly the glad song
of the angels—"Glory to God in the highest,
on earth peace and good will toward men."
The babe in swaddling clothes, type of their
own young lives, they feel is not a figure of
speech only, but a blessed reality. The rejoicing when the happy time comes, makes the
advent of Christmas welcome to all; and merry
groups may be seen going to and fro through
the streets, carrying the presents they have
received from their god-parents and friends,
and proudly showing them as trophies won by
good behavior. The frosty morning or even

chilling winter blasts do not deter them; and
if you go abroad, you see them everywhere.
Most of the children's gifts are received from
their god-parents. With the Germans this
relationship is a near one; it has more than
ordinary responsibility in it. When an infant
is baptized, the parents select two persons,
either from their kindred or friends. These
persons make a solemn vow at the altar that
they will perform the duties of parents to the
child in the event of the death of its natural
parents. This makes the tie a binding one,
and an affectionate interest is often the result.
god-parents usually participate in all the
pleasures of their little charges, and Christmas
is deemed a fitting time for them to show their
love and thoughtful consideration.

CHAPTER IV.

"When time, which steals our years away,
    Shall steal our pleasures too,
The memory of the past will stay
    And half our joys renew."

Moore.

"Oh! friends regretted, scenes forever dear,
    Remembrance hails you with her warmest tear;
Drooping, she bends o'er pensive Fancy's urn,
    To trace the hours which never can return."

Byron.

"Fond memory, to her duty true,
    Brings back their faded forms to view;
How lifelike, thro' the mist of years,
    Each well-remembered face appears."

Charles Sprague.

Parents in Germany are bound by law to send their children to school when they reach the age of six years. Twice a year days are appointed for their admission. These occur in the Spring and Autumn. The law is compulsory. No parent is allowed to keep his child at home to the neglect of his education. Sickness of the child itself is the only possible excuse admitted. In this way, all have an opportunity to learn. The neglect of a care-less, thoughtless, or even wofully indifferent parent is not permitted to interfere with the child's welfare, in this particular at least.

In thus giving the priceless boon of know-ledge, much is placed within reach of the recipient, that, in a multitude of instances, would never be hoped for, were not such pro-vision made. The law is of incalculable advantage to the youth of Germany, in furn-ishing incentives to all classes. Uprightness of character and a good education in the schools, form their models of excellence.

There can be no greater blessing for the masses than liberal and enlightened education. It can only elevate a community. Let schools be in any country what they should be, and prisons would be fewer.

I had often heard my brothers speak of school. I had waited with eager expectation to be old enough to accompany them. When a very little girl I loved to study. The school-room was, in my fancy, a sort of fairy kingdom, where all the pupils were dutiful subjects. I was six years old. At last school day had come for me. My dreams were to be realized or destroyed. I longed for the hour of starting.

When it was time to go, my heart seemed to quicken its beating, and my feet wanted to run.

It was a bright May day, and everything appeared to look glad and hopeful. Entering school with my brothers was the first marked event of my childlife—the very happiest experience. It promised to me, in my youthful imagination, only pleasure. The paths of knowledge, I thought, could only be flowery paths. Of the thorns hidden among the flowers I never dreamed. I did not suppose the hours could ever wearily drag their slow length along in a school-room.

It is well for us the future is unknown. Its hidden disappointments, discovered to us, would make existence only an endurance. The knowledge of what tests we are to pass through, the trials we are to endure, would paralyze the stoutest heart. God is wise in withholding from us the secrets of the years to come. He leads us on from infancy to old age, lifting our burdens if they are too heavy, or fitting us to bear them.

My eldest and second brothers, Andrew and Charles, were in the higher department. Brother Freddie and I entered the primary department,

4

as we were beginners. He was something older than I, and was farther advanced. No one noticed the little shy stranger as she entered. The children were very noisy. I grew tired of the confusion and wished myself home. So vanished my dream, touched by the wand of reality. My air-castles were fast tumbling into ruin. The fairy kingdom was not what I had fancied it. But soon the teacher made his appearance. In an instant everything was quiet. He bade all a hearty good morning, which the scholars returned with equal enthusiasm. Then observing me, he came and took my hand caressingly, and said he hoped I would be a good girl. He promised to be kind to me if I would be studious and obedient. I felt some of my castles still stood up, some of my dreams were coming true.

When I had imagined a character for the teacher, I had decided upon a personage invested with much dignity, and of whom I was to stand in great awe. I had made a character from my brothers' accounts, but I was wrong in all my conclusions. Mr. Uffelman was short in stature and young in years. I had imagined him tall, and old, and very grave. Instead of which he was lively and playful, except during school time. He seemed to me almost like myself—a little child.

This is a fortunate impression for a teacher to make. Confidence is at once secured, and the barrier thrown down separating the two relationships from each other. A child is far more easily taught if an affectionate interest can be secured. If the teacher possess inherent dignity, rather than that which the office bestows, there is little fear but what he will win his way to a child's heart, and yet control at the same time his wayward impulses.

There can be no healthy mental exercise, if dread of power only induce the performance of duty. There should always be perfect freedom of thought, if full development is the teacher's object. A judicious guide can check without discouraging the opening intellect, and thus prune or wisely direct any undesirable tendencies.

As I recall my first teacher, he was of pleasing appearance, calculated to win a child's admiration. His hair and eyes were dark, the latter with a merry twinkle in them. Very kindly eyes they were, as he smiled upon our childish efforts. His brow was high, broad and white, with waves of his dark hair falling

carelessly over it.   Though a very little girl, I
greatly admired this teacher, and now I think
of him as I knew him then, one of the best
and kindest friends I had.

School opened daily with the singing of a
morning hymn by the children, and the reading by the teacher of a portion of Scripture;
after these exercises, a prayer was repeated in
concert by the school.   Thus our thoughts
were directed to the Giver of all good, and we
were doubtless more dutiful and obedient for
this early morning sacrifice.

Our first lesson was in vocal music.   A full
hour was devoted to this study every day.
The teacher accompanied either with violin or
some other instrument.   Much attention is
paid to music in the schools.   It is, perhaps,
more thoroughly taught than any other of the
branches, excepting the elementary studies.
By this means a very creditable knowledge of
the art is obtained, which is not only a source
of pleasure, but becomes a source of profit as
well.   Many adopt the profession, and make a
comfortable living, either as musicians or teachers of the art.   There is probably a greater
number of Germans who are music teachers
than any other people, and this is owing, in a

great measure to the skill they acquire in the schools provided by the Government.

After our hour's music lesson, a period for recreation was allowed before another study was taken up. In this way the mind was relieved, and the next task was welcomed with zest and spirit. The day was varied all through, and at the close of school we felt almost as fresh as when it began. We experienced no sense of weariness or disgust from having been overworked. There had been no effort to cram our young brain; only enough had been done to stimulate and invigorate. It is the aim in these German schools to so regulate study and rest, that the body retain its due strength while the mind is being fed. Healthy minds and bodies with such a system observed, may be secured. There is no gorging permitted, even though the food be intellectual. As a result, the student on leaving school is matured mentally and physically, and not dwarfed in either respect.

The opinion is rapidly gaining ground everywhere, that, to be well taught, one must not necessarily be much taught. Thoughtful men and women are carefully studying the philanthropy as well as the philosophy of the school-room, and ere long noble examples of success, without the influence of the high pressure system, will appear. A thoroughly healthy and judicious mode of teaching will be established, and the errors of the past will be atoned for.

When I had been attending school two years, I was joined by my younger sister, Maria. We accompanied each other with glad hearts, for we were loving sisters. The way seemed shorter and brighter, and the school-room more attractive, now that she was to share with me its privileges. Brother Freddie had been promoted to the higher department. I should have missed him sadly, but my little sister now took his place, and was my companion at school.

I progressed in my studies under the faithful supervision of our teacher, and I shall ever feel grateful for the knowledge I gained while with him. Could I have lifted the veil behind which my future was hidden, and have known what was in store for me, I should, even as a little child, have applied myself more diligently. Not then had the slightest indication of the affliction I was to bear made appearance. I was a light-hearted, merry girl; but eight years had passed over my head, and no thought of sorrow had come to me. And yet there was a sad deprivation to be realized in a few years.

As I look back upon this period of my life when I saw the faces of those I loved, when I was permitted to look upon Nature, and take its beauties in through the outward vision, I think of precious opportunities not fully appreciated. Still I merited my teacher's approval. He sometimes told me my penmanship almost equalled his. This made me ambitious. I was proud that he thought well of me, and strove hard to continue to merit his good opinion.

CHAPTER V.

"Go forth into the fields;
Go forth, and know the gladness Nature yields.
 *   *   *   *   *   *
Hark! from each fresh-clad bough,
  Or blissful soaring in the air,
Bright birds, with joyous music, bid you now
  To the Spring's loved haunts repair."
W. J. Pabodie.

Now May, with life and music,
  The blooming valley fills,
And rears her flowery arches
  For all the little rills."
William Cullen Bryant.

Just after my sister started to school, a
general pic-nic was held. The schools of five
different villages participated. All were to
assemble at the appointed place, a beautiful
grove, about equally distant from each village.
The hour of starting was to be selected by each
school for itself, only all were to be together
for dinner.

The grove was a lovely spot, beautifully
shaded with high, over-arching trees. A limpid stream rippled out from a rock jutting

suddenly up from the ground, forming a natural fountain. Then the bright water emptied itself into a rivulet, which went singing its way along, following in its course the gently sloping ground, and, at a little distance off, quietly settled itself into a crystal lake.

The birds sang in the tree-tops, or flitted about among the boughs and branches. The grass was soft and velvety to the tread. Wild flowers were scattered everywhere, ready to hide themselves timidly away as the voices of children rang out on the air; fearing lest they should be ruthlessly trampled upon, or snatched from the embrace of the long meadow grass, to deck the hat of some fair village beauty.

The morning was clear; the sky so cloudless, promised a whole day of pleasure. King Sol had stepped forth from his chambers in the East in the best possible humor, and not even a fleecy spot was in all the heavens. The children saw this, and their hearts bounded with joy. Their light footsteps were the echoes of their excessive happiness.

According to the plan that had been arranged for them, the different schools started on their journey to the woods. Every child was full of expectation of promised pleasure. Bright

5

faces shone again, and ringing peals of laughter made the forests jubilant as the merry groups passed through them.

The scholars were to be in charge of the teachers, who were expected to conduct them safely to the pic-nic grounds. We started at the appointed hour, walked a long time, and yet did not seem to get any nearer our destination; as far as we could see, forests only were visible. We had expected to meet some of the other schools; but instead of doing so, we found ourselves close by the ruins of a city, without having seen the path leading to the grove we were seeking. We were lost! We were not alarmed, for we at least knew the way we had come, and could retrace our steps. We were all in excellent spirits, and were much amused at our mistake. Our teacher was a stranger, and had taken the wrong road. We were merry over the idea of probably having our pic-nic to ourselves.

Mr. Uffelman suggested we should eat our dinners. While doing so, he gave us an interesting account of ruins he had visited elsewhere. He pointed out any similarity between those and the ones we had so unexpectedly discovered. He narrated some stories of ancient ruined castles. Some of these were rather ghostly, but they were told in broad daylight, and we did not fear vexed spirits. We felt like searching among the few remaining shattered walls by which we were surrounded, to see if we could find any trace of the supernatural. But we contented ourselves with listening to the stories, and the moral which our teacher drew from each.

We enjoyed our dinner exceedingly. After it was over, we strolled on till we were beyond the ruins. We had begun to think we should entirely fail to find the other schools, and were wondering what would be thought of our not coming, when lo! we were in their very midst.

Our surprise was great, for we did not know we were near them. Everybody was glad to see us. We were asked innumerable questions, why we were so late arriving; where we had been; and if we had had our dinners. To all of which we gave satisfactory answers. It amused our friends very much that we should have lost our way. They laughed heartily at our mishap. Our greeting was all the more cordial as it had been so long deferred, and we entered with keen relish into all the sports of the occasion.

Never had I seen such a multitude of children. The number appeared too great to be counted. This impression was, of course, partly attributable to my inexperience. There were probably two thousand, as each school approximated four hundred scholars, and sometimes exceeded that number. We spent the remainder of the day rambling through the woods, swinging, jumping the rope, playing singing plays, dancing, and in every possible way in which children could be amused.

The time passed rapidly, and the day seemed short to us when the hour for our return arrived. We were called together, and a hymn was sung. The grove was filled with music, as the voices of two thousand happy children swelled forth in song. The birds were silent, and even the leaves and the little rivulet seemed to pause, that they might listen. Good-byes were exchanged, and each teacher, with his band of scholars, turned their steps towards home. The whole day was what the morning had promised, replete with pleasure.

With what delight in after life are recalled such pastimes as these. They often become the only bright tints in a heavily shaded life-picture. When all freshness of feeling has passed, and the heart is bowed in grief, how often have we seen the aged face relumed with joy at the remembrance of a butterfly chase, or some equally evanescent and swiftly vanishing joy.

When intervening years have been steeped in oblivion too dense for aught to penetrate it, the sports of childhood often come back, bringing with them a thrill of pleasure naught else can give. Why this is so, we may not clearly discern. Perhaps because they were first impressions, they took deeper hold upon the fancy. Or as the world, with its busy cares, had not then divided the heart's affections, these loves of childhood may have been more precious to gentle memory, and she hid them away for the retrospection of later years. Whatever may be the reason, we are every day reminded how very dear, even when feeble steps are tottering on the brink of the grave, are the reminiscences of earliest years.

From my infancy I have been passionately fond of music. When I was about seven years of age, a musical entertainment was to be given by the people of a neighboring town, an hour's walk distant. I had heard much talk concerning the intended jubilee, and everything I heard interested me greatly. I became very anxious to attend. I could think of nothing else for days before, and when the time arrived, I was in a feverish state of excitement. Whit Monday had been appointed for the entertainment. Many people were going from our village. At the hour for starting, I left the house without my parents' knowledge, and followed a party bound for the *fête*. Soon after reaching the grounds, I lost sight of the familiar faces of persons from my home, and found myself surrounded by strangers. I did not feel afraid, so intent was I upon the full enjoyment of the music.

The entertainment took place in a park just beneath a gracefully sloping hill. It was well shaded, and beautifully laid out in flower beds and gravelled walks. It also contained several pavilions, in which were tables filled with a variety of refreshment. I soon found a group of children playing by a pretty brook. They were pulling bulrushes and plaiting them; then making little fancy wreaths and baskets, and enjoying themselves finely. I, of course, was attracted. Children soon become acquainted. In a little while I was perfectly at home with my new-found friends, and we had a joyous time. Dinner was announced by the sounding of a silver horn. The parents of my playmates invited me to dine with them. I must have seemed very lonely, but I did not feel so. I spent the day delightfully, without a thought of my home, or the distance I was from it.

About sunset I began to think of my long walk back. I could not find the persons I had come with. I became alarmed. I wondered what my father and mother would say to me; what I should tell them, and if they would punish me. These were not very agreeable reflections after a day of pleasure. But I had left without the knowledge or consent of my parents, and was now dreading the deserved penalty of disobedience. I had been well trained, and thought of no way of escape but to tell the truth, and ask to be forgiven. I had done wrong I knew, and believed I should receive the merited consequences of my fault. My walk home was very lonely It was growing towards night, and I recalled all the ghost stories I had ever heard. Every sound made me quicken my steps. I fancied strange sights all along the road, and ran as fast as I could, till I had to slacken my pace to rest; then would run again, almost breathless with fright.

At last I reached home, without having been devoured by goblins or wicked elves of any kind. Father and mother were much surprised when I told them my day's adventures. They were astonished to learn I had come back alone, and were glad no mischance had overtaken their erring child. They supposed I had gone to spend the day with one of my schoolmates, and would be brought home by some older member of the family. They cautioned me against going such a distance again without gaining their permission. They chid me very gently, and did not punish me severely, as I had expected they would. It was my first offence, so they forgave me. I shall never forget how grateful I felt to be allowed to give and receive the usual good-night kiss.

My stolen pleasures were sweet while being enjoyed, but brought after regret. Had not my kind parents forgiven me, I should have been a miserable little girl when I laid my head on my pillow. As it was, with an unburdened heart and a weary body, I was soon sound asleep, snugly stowed away in my comfortable bed, to dream, perhaps, of my wanderings, the lonely forest walk, my dread of a reprimand, but to linger last and longest on the sweet seal of pardon—the good-night kiss of my parents.

CHAPTER VI.

"All places that the eye of heaven visits,
Are to a wise man ports and happy havens."
Shaks. Richard II.

"Mother, how still the baby lies!
I cannot hear his breath;
I cannot see his laughing eyes—
They tell me this is death."
Mrs. Gilman.

"There is a voice I shall hear no more;
There are tones whose music for me is o'er,
Sweet as the odors of Spring were they—
Precious and rich, but they died away;
They came like peace to my heart and ear,
Ne'er again will they murmur here;
They have gone like the blush of a summer moon,
Like a crimson cloud through the sunset borne."
W. G. Clarke.

At this time my father was constantly receiving letters from his brother, who had settled in America, urging him to dispose of his property and emigrate with his family. My parents could not make up their minds to leave their native land. But my uncle continued to write, earnestly advising them to do so. Finally, after long reflection, my father and mother thought that as they had a large family, the new world might possess advantages for their children which their own country did not. So after much consideration, and with some misgivings, they concluded at the expiration of four months to leave for America. It was quite a serious undertaking, but it appeared providential for them to go. We began making the necessary preparations for our departure. All was bustle in our home. Mother's face was anxious, but she would not allow herself to regret the step she had decided to take. If her children's good was to be secured, she was willing to make any sacrifice. She believed it was for the best, and all other considerations were nobly set aside. Such is a mother's love. She knows no aim but the welfare of her family.

All were busy, getting ready to cross the briny deep. Even the children were doing what they could, when, as though to remind us how vain are all our plans if God should see fit to interpose and stay them, our darling little brother Louis sickened and died. This was a sad blow. Mother feared it might be ominous that our going to America was not a wise decision. He was but four years old, our

household pet, his winning ways our constant
pleasure. Yet God took the blossom from us
to bloom where no blight could destroy its
beauty; and the little one laid in his grave
across the ocean, often when we were settled in
our new home, made us wander back to the
land we had left. A tie was formed that no
change of scene or circumstance could break.
We love the spot with green turf above it,
where sleep those we tenderly cherish. And
in waking dreams, or when slumber's soft
mantle has enfolded the senses, we often linger
there.

I was greatly delighted at the idea of going
to America. It was to me a wonderful place.
I had heard so much about it, that I thought it
must surely be a better world than I had lived
in, its fruits more luscious, its flowers more
lovely, and its people more famous. Like
stories told me of Aladdin's lamp and its magical
power, were the accounts of this new land.
Very marvellous were my childish imaginations. I could scarcely study my lessons after
it had been determined we were to go. My
thoughts were almost exclusively upon the
prospects before us. My teacher would pat
me on the cheek and say laughingly, " Oh,

you think too much about America; you will not find it so very wonderful."

A few days before taking leave of our friends, sister and myself met Mr. Uffelman. He asked us "if we were in a hurry to get home." We told him "no." He desired us to return with him to his home. We accompanied him, and found he had prepared a nice little parting treat for us. We were both surprised and pleased at his thoughtfulness. He told us he was on his way to our home when he met us. We had left school a short time before, and so had not seen him daily, as we had been accustomed to. Sister and I were delighted with this pleasant surprise, and were not likely ever to forget it.

It takes only a little thing to gratify children. They magnify all kindnesses, and in their generosity are sure to make large returns of love and confidence. No matter how desolate or lonely we may be, we may always win the affection of a child; and it is very pure, worthier to have and hold than that of persons older grown, if with the latter self interest add a feather weight in the scale.

Our teacher talked with us of our intended journey. He told us in the country to which

we were going people were not always as strict
in their notions of duty as they should be. In
their haste to become rich, parents frequently
were regardless of their children's interests,
and removed them when very young from
school to aid in making money. The children
were glad to get rid of study, and were very
willing to give up school. In this way they
began to be men and women in their notions,
while they still were children in years. This,
he thought, was in a measure owing to the fact
that many persons had emigrated to America
with the sole object of accumulating wealth.
The country was young; its agriculture, mineral
and mechanical resources were abundant. It
was, indeed, in the opinion of some a land of
gold, and their purpose in seeking it was to
become possessed of a goodly share of the
precious commodity. His theory may not have
been a correct one in every respect; it may
have been in a degree exaggerated; yet I have
since found it was not wholly without founda-
tion. There is an eagerness for mere worldly
gain that does interfere with higher and less
perishable attainments. But the country is
growing older; and with plenty in her right
hand, she still may take hold of wisdom's

sceptre, and while not neglecting opportunities to possess wealth, yet not make it the one aim of a life.

Mr. Uffelman counselled us to continue at school as long as our parents could possibly permit us. He hoped we would remain at least till we were confirmed. By that time we should have acquired a fair education, and be ready creditably to do our part in the world. He then bade us good-bye, and we parted from our friend and teacher, never again to meet on earth.

The day came on which we were to quit the home of our first years. We were to leave forever behind us the land of our birth. We should never tread its soil again. We children were very young, but the subdued grief of our parents impressed us, and we understood it was no ordinary change we were making. It is true our parting was not altogether sorrowful, for we were very hopeful as to what our new home would prove to be. Our anticipations were bright, and our regrets were principally that we were leaving friends and neighbors, to whom we were fondly attached. Our playmates were sad at the thought of our going so far away. Many of them with tearful eyes pre-

sented mementos of their affection. These
little gifts, love-tokens as they surely were, were
dearly prized. The last good-byes were spoken.
We looked back upon our pleasant home, then
turned from it forever, followed by the "God
speed" of the dear ones who had remained
longest with us.

My mother's parting request, as she bade
her sister farewell, was in memory of the little
one she had so recently put away, asleep in his
new-made grave. She begged that flowers
might be kept blooming above the cherished
form—violet, and hyacinth, and sweet-scented
rose,—and mingling with them the mourning
cypress, emblems of his youth and loveliness,
and her sorrowing heart. She felt that although
his body was in the grave, yet the spirit had
winged its flight to realms of endless life. The
fleshy tabernacle would become food for worms,
but he was where "neither moth nor rust doth
corrupt." He was beyond the skies, himself
a cherub among the angels and bright-winged
seraphs. His voice, never again to be broken
into infant wailing, would forever burst forth
into song, "Hosanna to the Lord," the burden
of the melody.

Lips that had just learned to lisp "mother,"

here on earth, would, in heaven, welcome that
mother with a glad "All hail," when she,
having done with earth's toils, should again
fold her darling in her fond embrace.

"No bitter tears be shed,
    Blossom of being, seen and gone;
With flowers alone we strew thy bed,
    O blest departed one!
Whose all of life—a rosy ray,
Blush'd into dawn, and passed away.

Yes, thou art fled, ere guilt had power
    To stain thy cherub-soul and form,
Closed is the soft ephemeral flower,
    That never felt a storm!
The sunbeam's smile, the zephyr's breath,
All that it knew from life to death.

Thou wert so like a form of light,
    That heaven benignly called thee hence,
Ere yet the world could breathe one blight
    O'er thy sweet innocence.
And thou, that brighter home to bless,
Art passed, with all thy loveliness!

Oh! hadst thou still on earth remained,
    Vision of beauty, fair as brief;
How soon thy brightness had been stain'd
    With passion or with grief!
Now not a sullying breath can rise,
To dim thy glory in the skies.

We rear no marble o'er thy tomb,
    No sculptur'd image there shall mourn;

Ah! fitter far the vernal bloom
  Such dwelling to adorn.
Fragrance, and flowers, and dews must be
The only emblems meet for thee.

Thy grave shall be a blessed shrine,
  Adorn'd with Nature's brightest wreath,
Each glowing season shall combine
  Its incense there to breathe;
And oft upon the midnight air
Shall viewless harps be murmuring there.

And oh! sometimes in visions blest,
  Sweet spirit visit our repose,
And bear from thine own world of rest
  Some balm for human woes.
What form more lovely could be given,
Than thine, to be messenger of heaven?"

To us as children, our leaving Germany did
not seem to have any special significance. We
soon forgot, in the excitement of travel, our
sorrow, and were ready to enjoy everything.
We had no forebodings, no anxieties. We were
going in a few days to take up our abode, for some
weeks at least, in a big ship,—as big as a house.
We thought this very novel, and were full of
wonderment as to how everything would be.
Our speculations, could they have been set
down, would have been most amusing. Our
buoyant expectations cheered our parents, and
6

they endeavored to consider without regret the step they had taken. Their trust was in God, who is always strong to deliver, even if erring human judgment prove unwise.

> There is a pow'r our path to guide,
>   E'en though a thorny way;
> Our God is just, whate'er betide,
>   He can all evil stay.
>
> We must trust His pow'r divine,
>   Lean on His strong right arm;
> He'll make His light to shine,
>   And lead us from all harm.

CHAPTER VII.

"Let us depart! the universal sun
 Confines not to one land his blessed beams."
                                    Southey's Madoc.

"Come, fair repentance, daughter of the skies,
 Soft harbinger of soon returning virtue;
 The weeping messenger of grace from heav'n!"
                                    Brown's Athelstan.

"Fare thee well! the ship is ready,
   And the breeze is fresh and steady;
   Hands are fast the anchor weighing,
   High in air the streamers playing.
   Spread the sails, the waves are swelling
   Proudly round thy buoyant dwelling.
   Fare thee well, and when at sea,
   Think of those who sigh for thee!"
                                    Hannah F. Gould.

Two days' delightful travel brought us to
Bremen. It was late in the evening when we
arrived. After partaking of a refreshing supper,
we retired. Next morning father took us out
for a walk. We were anxious to see the place.
We found it a city of considerable commercial importance, situated on the river Weser;
famous for its wine cellars. These are divided

into compartments: in one of which are the wine casks called " The Rose," and " The Twelve Apostles." These names are traditional, and are appropriately significant. Much store is set upon their possession.

The Cathedral is a Gothic building of the twelfth century. It is well preserved, and is unique and suggestive in structure. It bears marks of its great age in the various growth that has clung to its time-honored walls, and which has in places turned to fossil, and become a part of the stone. Quaint devices have in this way been traced on wall, and frieze and cornice. The antiquated pile is eloquent, though voiceless in its grandeur, " speaking of the past unto the present." It has a language of its own unwritten and unspoken, but holding communion with the heart of man.

The vault of the church has the property of preserving the bodies of the dead from decomposition. This is curious, but it is nevertheless true. The idea may have been taken from the ancient Egyptian method of embalming the dead, and then placing them in an atmosphere where they remain in the same condition for ages.

We found many other interesting things in

Bremen; none, however, more so than the wine cellars and the cathedral, and none that were remarkable enough for us to spend much time in visiting. We were pleased with all we saw—although our stay was brief.

The greater number of Germans emigrating to America, embark at this point. Vessels of large size stop at Bremen haven, near the mouth of the river Weser. Two fine bridges connect the banks of this river. These add to the business facilities of the city, and are sources of wealth to the people.

On our return from our walk and sight-seeing, we took dinner. There was a large number of guests at the hotel; and after dinner they were scattered through the house, apparently enjoying themselves very much, all according to their several fancies. Some were chatting, others reading, and groups were engaged in various parlor games. I was feeling rather lonely, as I had become accidentally separated from my family. While sitting, watching what was going on around me, a strange lady came and took a seat by my side. She asked me some questions: who I was, where I was from, and if I was going to remain long in Bremen.

To this last inquiry I answered, "I did not know, as I had not heard my parents say." She seemed interested in me, and I was pleased with the attention she paid me. She desired me to ask my mother if I might accompany her home for a short visit. I left her to find mother. When at her door, I thought she surely would not let me go, as the lady was an entire stranger. I had taken a great liking to my new friend, and wished exceedingly to go with her. I concluded it would not be very wrong to go without my mother's permission, as I should be gone only a little while. I decided to return and say I had my mother's consent to do as she wished me. I was tempted to deceive, and yielded. I thought my parents would not care. I forgot for the moment the oft repeated counsel I had received; never to tell an untruth, that harm would surely follow.

I acted according to the impulses of my sinful, selfish heart. I told the lady I could go, and went with her to her home. She was kind and loving to me; she petted and caressed me in the fondest manner, and I was completely captivated. I remained all night with my new acquaintance. I was so pleased, I forgot my disobedience, and thought only of present happiness. Next day we went visiting, and had a pleasant time; then we returned to the hotel. What was my surprise, to find my parents, brothers and sisters had gone. I became greatly alarmed. My friend took me to the proprietor of the hotel. My dismay can hardly be imagined, when he told me all my family had left that morning on their voyage to America. The ship was starting in which they were to sail, and they were compelled to go. He thought my father had found me, as he had not seen him for some hours. I burst into tears. I thought my heart would break. I was utterly miserable. Everybody tried to comfort me, but I was inconsolable. I was a hopeless desolate child. I had been very wicked, and this was my punishment. It seemed greater than I could bear. I remembered my folly in deep contrition, and was truly penitent, but this did not restore me to my parents; and my sorrow was unabated.

Mrs. Kiester did everything she could to allay my grief, but all her efforts failed, till she happened to say she expected to go to America in a short time, and she would take me with her, and we would try our utmost to find my parents. I returned with her to her home a

sadder and wiser child. I was not likely ever
again to deceive.

Two days passed; I heard nothing of my
parents. On the evening of the second day,
sick and weary, I retired early, to ponder on
my forlorn situation—a deserted child, among
entire strangers. When just as I laid down, I
heard a familiar voice in the hall; it was my
father's. I leaped out of bed, ready to dance
for joy, and in an instant was folded in his
arms. I was at first afraid he would be dis-
pleased with me, and would chide me severely
for the trouble and anxiety I had caused him;
but Mrs. Kiester interceded for me, explained
everything, and shared the blame. She had
asked me to go with her, not knowing the
family were to leave Bremen so soon. Very
earnest were her efforts to reconcile my father
to my misconduct, in having gone away without his or my mother's consent. Her excuse
was, I was too young to reflect how wrong it
was to do so; she felt sure I would never repeat
the offence. Father listened to her pleading
in my behalf, and kindly forgave me.

He told us how alarmed he was when, just
as he was starting, I could nowhere be found.
He thought I must have strayed away and lost

myself. He had purchased tickets for the family on the first ship out. This was to leave the day after I left the hotel with my stranger friend. He took the family to the point from which the ship was to start, then returned to seek his missing child. He could learn nothing of my whereabouts. I had not told any one where I was going; this rendered search for me fruitless. I resolved never again to distress my parents by being disobedient and untruthful. The circumstance made a lasting impression upon me. Ever after, if I felt like equivocating in the slightest, I recalled with a shudder, the agony I endured, and the remembrance prevented my sinning again in the same way. If a child should read my simple story, I would urge that, under all temptation, the truth be told. Very few possibly, will pass through the ordeal I did, but falsehood will always bring its own bitter penalty.

Father and I left for Bremen port next day. My mother met me, as soon as we reached the place where she had been waiting for me. Words cannot express her delight when she saw her little daughter Mary. She threw her arms around me and wept for joy. She had dreaded having to leave the country without

7

finding me. Father intended to stay and search for me, and have mother and the other children go without him. He and I would follow as soon as he had found me. My mother's anguish had been intense. She felt she would rather have laid me beside my little brother Louis, than perhaps never to know what had become of me. We told mother all about Mrs. Kiester, how she had fascinated me, and how frightened I had been when I could not find my parents. Mother laughed and cried during the narrative, and when it was ended she mildly reproved my thoughtlessness. She told me she was deeply grieved that I had told a falsehood; but she forgave me, and we were once more a united family; the one stray lamb had been brought back into the fold.

The vessel in which we were to sail had already moved out a short distance from the shore, so father had to procure a small boat in which we might be conveyed to it.

Just as we were seated in the boat, father missed my sister Maria. There was momentary alarm, for mother feared she might have fallen into the water unobserved. Our anxiety was, however, fortunately this time but of short duration; for looking to a little distance, father saw her busily playing with a group of children. We soon had her with us, and had a hearty laugh beside at our unnecessary alarm.

When we were all on board, and the vessel struck out for the open sea, she appeared like a thing of life. The people on shore looked on admiringly; the scene was indeed most enlivening. The good ship seemed like a bird on the ocean wave; gaily she flapped her sails as the wind filled them. Now she rose on the breast of a billow; then dipped down into the briny tide. We enjoyed the sensation.

CHAPTER VIII.

"Adieu, adieu! my native shore
    Fades o'er the waters blue;
The night winds sigh, the breakers roar,
    And shrieks the wild sea-mew.
Yon sun that sets upon the sea,
    We follow in his flight:
Farewell awhile to him and thee,
    My native land, good-night."

                                    Byron.

"The uptorn waves rolled hoar and huge;
    The far-thrown undulations
Swelled out in the sun's last lingering smile,
    And fell like battling nations."

                                J. O. Rockwell.

"A sound comes on the rising breeze,
    A sweet and lovely sound;
Piercing the tumult of the seas
    That wildly dash around.

From land, from sunny land it comes,
    From hills with murmuring trees,
From paths by still and happy homes—
    That sweet sound on the breeze."

                                Felicia Hemans.

The ship in which we sailed was of the
largest kind, and was named after the river

Weser. There were on board between two and three hundred passengers, one-third of whom were Jews. In a few days we lost sight of beautiful Germany, the land of our birth; our Fatherland. It faded from our vision like a speck on the horizon, as we followed in the sun's path to seek our home in the far off West. Even the youngest of our number waited and watched till land could no longer be seen; and sea and sky alone were visible.

We saw tears in our mother's eyes. She remembered friends left behind, and felt we were going a long way to make new ones. We, too, were ready to weep, thinking of the companions we were never more to meet. But father kept a brave heart, and spoke cheering words to us, which made smiles come and chase the tears away.

Childhood's heart, like the violet-eyed helio-trope, turns ever to the sun. Sorrow beyond its years may weigh it down, but let the sunlight look in, and straightway its chambers are full of light. We were soon well pleased with our home on the deep blue sea. We visited every part of the big ship, and were wonderfully curious concerning everything about it. There were no resources we did not discover.

We asked innumerable questions as to what each meant, what its purpose was, and all else a child's busy brain could think of.

The experiences of the first few weeks were pleasant. There were calm moonlight nights. These were far more weird and fascinating than moonlight nights on land. At least so we children thought, and we loved to stay up late and watch the silvery matron as she dived down into the ocean, or rested in calm serenity on its bosom. Music and dancing gave to the evening hours a rapid flight. Our amusements in the day time were looking for immense fish, watching the sailors as they climbed to the masthead, or attended to the various work on board ship. We made friends with the captain and steward, with the latter rather more particularly, as occasionally he treated us to lumps of sugar and other good things.

After four weeks of pleasant weather, our enjoyments were broken in upon by a severe storm, which lasted three days and nights. All this time we were enveloped in a heavy mist; this became so dense that the sky was dark as night; it hid everything from view. " There was not a clear speck in heaven," save when the lightning flashed. For an instant,

then, there would be zigzag gleams of light,
that made the darkness more fearful. The
thunder crashed, making the vault of heaven
hideous with wild reverberations. The mad
waves lashed each other into fury. The
children crouched in terror close to their
parents. All was consternation and dismay,
for danger seemed inevitable. But Providence interposed, as in days of old; He bade
the turbulent sea "peace be still," and the
angry storm subsided. Its sobbings died off
in the distance. The sky again was clear, and
the voice of the winds sank low as a gentle
lullaby song.

A lovely rainbow was stretched across the
heavens. We knew this was a promise of fair
weather. We remembered it was God's cove-
nant with man when another and fiercer storm
swept over land and sea, and earth was deluged
in its wrath. The ark reminded us of our own
good ship. It reached Mount Ararat, and
rested there in safety, and the bow was in the
clouds, a promise of protection. We thought
our bark would reach its destined port, and we
should see God's smile in the sky.

There was a great variety of people on board
ship. Young as I was, I noticed many pecu-

liarities; some in disposition, some in manner, and some in outward appearance. A sea voyage furnishes admirable opportunity of observing character. It is an old saying, "to know people well, you should live with them;" and though I was a child, I would sit for hours making studies of the persons by whom I was surrounded. A child's perceptions, though immature, are acute, if not always accurate. Its preference generally indicates the possession of good and noble traits by the individual preferred. Their nervous sensibility is true, if no higher medium be the avenue leading to their friendships. We have often observed a charming exterior repulse a child, while absolute deformity has attracted. This is because the homely exterior was the garb of a true heart, and the child readily discerned it. The expression is often heard—it is a good sign to be loved by the children.

During the weeks that intervened before we again saw land, we found many kind friends among the passengers, and we had many favorites. They entertained us with the telling of interesting and amusing stories. These would excite great wonder; but more frequently unbounded mirth, and peals of ringing, musical laughter, would be heard all over the ship.

It afforded infinite pleasure to every one to see us grouped, eager listeners, while these marvellous stories were being told. Some of them were of the new country to which we were going. Astonishing things were narrated, and we were very credulous, but sometimes they were so highly colored, that we knew they were manufactured at the time for our amusement. The cook would paint his face black, and tell us that he looked like all the Americans did. That when we had been there long enough, we would turn black too. This puzzled us greatly, for he told the story with a grave face, and we feared it might be true.

The captain also would occasionally join in our sports. He would throw handsful of raisins and prunes over the deck, and have us all scampering to pick them up. We would laugh and shout, and he would be equally merry. We considered this rare fun. In this way the tedium of a long voyage was lessened, and our trip made very pleasant to think upon in the future.

We had some discomfitures, as well as the older travellers. We were nearly all sea-sick. As the vessel would rock and plunge, our sensations were anything but agreeable. Sometimes we felt that we would rather die than live. But we encountered only one severe storm, and very little blustering weather; so we could not complain. Our few disagreeable experiences made the pleasant ones all the more acceptable.

During the journey I had one annoyance; my eyes became terribly inflamed. I did not at first mind it; I thought it would pass off soon. But the trouble increased, and assumed a virulent form. Everything was done to allay it, but without success. It was a continued source of pain; still we thought it temporary, and my parents were not uneasy. The physician on board thought the irritation resulted from having bathed my eyes in salt water. The result, however, proved more serious than had been anticipated.

The affliction, slight as it appeared, was the forerunner of disease that no skill could remedy. I did not dream of this for a moment. I was gradually prepared for the loss I was to sustain. Had this not been so, I could not have borne the trial. For years this one shadow was slowly but surely stealing across my path. Yet when it had fallen so deeply that no light could penetrate it, I was sadly stricken. But I will not anticipate.

When we had been eight weeks on the sea, we came in sight of land. The shores at first appeared like a dark thread along the horizon. Then the outline became clearer. We watched intensely, as objects one after another became defined. It seemed to us the land of promise. All were in excellent spirits, for we had come through great peril, and were thankful for the near prospect of being on land again.

The children were gathered on deck, eagerly looking on, when suddenly they shouted, "See, see, there are the black people the cook told us of!" Sure enough, there they were, a number of them, coming towards the vessel in small schooners. The sight to us was a novel one. We began to think the stories we had heard about the people in America were true. Some of us feared we might turn black too, as we had been told we should, when we had been long enough in the country. The older people were amused at our consternation. They told us they thought the cook must have meant the Indians, when he said the Americans were all black; or that he was joking with us, trying to see how much he could make us believe. We were much interested in the coal black shiny faces before us, and gazed at them as long as we had the opportunity.

Four days after our first sight of land, our vessel arrived safe in port. It was early on Sunday morning. As soon as we were on shore, we returned thanks to God, for His merciful preservation, and sang a hymn of praise.

When we tried to walk, we found ourselves unable to do so without swaying from side to side. We could scarcely stand upright; when we endeavored to do so, we felt as if we should surely fall down. We had become accustomed to the motion of the ship, and in spite of all our efforts, we would rock as it had done when bearing us o'er the bright blue sea. In a few days, however, we managed to overcome this undulating tendency, and walked very well for people who had not been on *terra firma* for so long a time.

CHAPTER IX.

"The hearth of home has a constant flame,
    And pure as vestal fire;
'Twill burn, 'twill burn, forever the same,
    For Nature feeds the pyre."
Mrs. Hale.

"Affliction is the wholesome soil of virtue;
Where patience, honor, sweet humanity,
Calm fortitude, take root and strongly flourish."
Mallet.

"Thou bright and star-like spirit,
    That in my visions mild,
I see 'mid heaven's seraphic host—
    O, canst thou be my child?

Thy feeble feet, unsteady,
    That tottered as they trod,
With angels walk the heavenly paths,
    Or stand before their God."
Thomas Ward.

We landed in Baltimore, a thriving, prosperous city, whose open port promised then to vie with those of older fame. This promise has not failed; it has been proved she has great advantages for commercial purposes. We remained here only two days, a too short time to see much of the city or to become acquainted with the people. Everything we saw or heard impressed us favorably. The monument in memory of George Washington we thought imposing and very beautiful. The shaft, in its great height typifying the lofty character of the Father of his Country, appeared to us a most fitting memorial. At least, when it had been explained to us how good and great a man it honored, we realized this as far as children might be expected to; not with so large an appreciation as older persons, of course. We have since learned to estimate for ourselves the wonderful combination of virtues found in this man. We are reminded here of many tributes paid his memory, for in every land his praise has been sung.

We find, perhaps, the greatest force and the truest portraiture from an English lady's gifted pen. She gives the first place among heroes to America's noble son. We will quote a part of her eloquent thought:—

"Rome had its Cæsar, great and brave, but stain was
　　on his wreath;
He lived the heartless conqueror, and died the tyrant's
　　death.

France had its Eagle; but his wings, though lofty
    they might soar,
Were spread in false ambition's flight, and dipped in
    murder's gore.
Those hero-gods, whose mighty sway would fain have
    chained the waves,
Who fleshed their blades with tiger zeal, to make a
    world of slaves,
Who, though their kindred barred the path, still fiercely
    waded on;
Oh, where shall be *their* 'glory' by the side of Wash-
    ington!

He fought, but not with love of strife; he struck but
    to defend;
And ere he turned a people's foe, he sought to be a
    friend.
He strove to keep his country's right by reason's gentle
    word,
And sighed when fell injustice threw the challenge-
    sword to sword.
He stood the firm, the calm, the wise, the patriot and
    the sage;
He showed no deep, avenging hate, no burst of despot
    rage.
He stood for liberty and truth, and dauntlessly led on,
Till shouts of victory gave forth the name of Wash-
    ington."

But all enconium is vain to give the simple
grandeur of a character such as his: the heart of
the people makes each its estimate, and offers
its meed of worship.

We thought Baltimore must be a pleasant place to live in, not bustling and noisy, nor over-given to business.

Sociality seemed a predominant element. The people were hospitable and kind. They were moderate in their modes of living, compared with residents of other cities of equal pretensions. These views I have heard my parents frequently express as their first impressions of Baltimore, and I have since found them correct, from my own observation. We liked the place and people exceedingly.

Our sight-seeing over, we left for Middletown, Frederick county, Maryland, sixty miles distant. My father's brother had settled there soon after he reached America. We spent a few very pleasant days with my uncle's family, talking of everything connected with our former home, recalling many persons and events almost forgotten by those who were now so removed from them.

Father rented a house in the village. When we had moved into it, we felt that we were once more in our own home. We had passed through various trials, and it was delightful to us to be again quietly settled. There was relief in the very idea, and a feeling of repose that we had not known for months. The villagers were kind in many ways. They could not understand our language, nor we their's; still they aided us greatly. They had a disposition to be of service, and words were not necessary. When the heart is kindly disposed, all obstacles may be overcome. Generous feelings will always find expression, even though it be but with the ready hand, or friendly smile. "Actions speak louder than words" is a true saying, which has lost none of its force in its time-worn usage.

As soon after we were settled as my father's pressing business duties would permit, he called in a physician to examine my eyes. They had been growing worse instead of better. They were inflamed and painful. I could use them but little without acute suffering. Dr. Smith examined them carefully, and pronounced the disease a severe form of ophthalmia, which, he feared, could not be arrested. He did not think my sight was in danger, but I should always have weak vision, owing to the inflammation having assumed a chronic form. He pronounced one eye more seriously affected than the other, still thought the sight of one was strong, and not likely to be impaired. This was encourag-

8

ing intelligence, for we had now begun to dread my going blind.

In order to prevent the inflammation spreading, Dr. Smith put a seton in the back of my neck. This was to remain there three months. It was very painful, but I strove to bear it patiently, as there was a fearful possibility, if the doctor's advice were not followed strictly.

Father thought it best at once to place my brothers at trades. He succeeded in accomplishing his wishes, satisfactorily to himself and to them also. Two went about fifteen miles from home, and one found employment in the village. My two younger sisters and myself remained at home to attend school. Many strange conjectures were indulged in respecting the new school. We wondered if it would be like the one in Deisel; if the teacher would be as good and kind, and as good looking; if we should see any faces blackened like the cook's, when he got himself up for our amusement; these, and many other foolish things were in our thoughts, as the time for going approached.

As soon as mother had made some necessary arrangements, we started. We found it very like the one we had attended. We saw no black faces, only bright sunny ones—rosy and laughing—just such as we had often seen before. We did not feel that we were in a strange place, but quite at home, more so perhaps, than we had felt since we were last in a similar place. We recalled a band of happy children and a kind teacher in a land beyond the sea, and hoped our present associations would prove just as pleasant.

We had been taught the English alphabet since our arrival in Middletown, by our Sunday school teacher, Miss Elizabeth Young. This lady had endeared herself to us by her winning ways, and the interest she felt in our advancement. It was fortunate for us that we had learned even the alphabet of the language which we were to speak. We felt less embarrassment, than if we had been utterly ignorant. We remembered with gratitude the assistance we had received. Our friend had not thought of the service her instruction would be to us.

When I had been in school about eight months, my eyes grew much worse. They were weaker, and sometimes I could scarcely see at all. This interfered greatly with my improvement. I made little if any progress. One day the teacher, Mr. Haupt, said to me, "Mary, you do not read as well now as you did six weeks ago." I had not told him with what difficulty I could see at all. My eyes appeared no more inflamed than they had for some time, and he was surprised that I did not improve, as he knew me to be studious.

My spirits were depressed. I had no heart for work of any sort, as everything cost me so great an effort. I could not bear to talk of my affliction, therefore endured a great deal of pain without speaking of it. The grief is heaviest of which we cannot speak. For our lighter sorrows we may ask sympathy, but if we have irremediable sorrow, the heart will hide it away, and the lips will be silent.

For months an indefinable dread had been hanging over me. It began now to take form, and I knew a severe calamity was in store for me. No one looked or spoke hopefully, when the condition of my eyes was the subject of conversation. When I turned to those I loved, their faces were sad. This was confirmation for my worst fears. I could not be light-hearted or gay, as other children were. I would often steal away from my companions, and go off by myself to weep. I strove to overcome these feelings; struggled hard to reason with myself, how foolish it was; but all to no avail; the pall was settling on my life, and I could not help grieving.

Mother at this time was often more quiet than usual. When asked why this was so, she reminded us that the anniversary of the death of our little brother Louis would soon occur.

She had not forgotten the little sleeper; and as the merry Christmas time approached, her thoughts wandered to the land where her babe was buried. Her heart echoed the tender musings of the poet, as she thought of her child—one year in heaven.

"One year among the angels, beloved, thou hast been;
  One year has heaven's white portal shut back the sound
      of sin:
  And yet no voice, no whisper, comes floating down
      from thee,
  To tell us what glad wonder a year of heaven may be.

  Our hearts before it listen,—the beautiful closed gate,
  The silence yearns around us; we listen as we wait.
  It is thy heavenly birthday, on earth thy lilies bloom;
  In thine immortal garland canst find for these no
      room?

  Thou lovedst all things lovely when walking with us
      here;
  Now from the height of heaven seems earth no longer
      dear?
  We cannot paint thee moving in white robed state
      afar,

Nor dream our flower of comfort, a cool and distant
    star.

Heaven is but life made richer; there can be no loss;
To meet our love and longing thou hast no gulf to
    cross;
No adamant between us uprears its rocky screen;
A veil before us only, thou in the light serene.

That veil 'twixt earth and heaven a breath might
    waft aside;
We breathe one air, beloved, we follow one dear Guide:
Passed into open vision, out of our mists and rain,
Thou seest how sorrow blossoms; how peace is won
    from pain.

As half we feel thee leaning from thy deep calm of
    bliss,
To say of earth, 'Beloved, how beautiful it is!
The lilies in this splendor, the green leaves in this
    dew;
O earth is also heaven, with God's light clothed anew!'

So when the sky seems bluer, and when the blossoms
    wear
Some tender, mystic shading, we never knew was there,
We'll say, 'We see things earthly by light of cherub-
    eyes;
He bends where we are gazing to-day, from Paradise.'

Because we know thee near us, and nearer still to
    Him
Who fills thy cup of being with glory to the brim;
We will not stain with grieving our fair, though fainter
    light,
But cling to thee in spirit, as if thou wert in sight.

And as in waves of beauty the swift years come and
    go,
Upon celestial currents our deeper life shall flow;
Hearing from that sweet country where blighting never
    came,
Love chime the hours immortal, in earth and heaven
    the same."

We shared with our mother her loving recol-
lection of our little brother, but we felt he was
happy, and did not mourn. It was the first
Christmas since his heaven-life began. We
should miss him from our sports. But our
household pet was at home "in a mansion not
made with hands," where, if we led holy lives,
we should again see him, with no fear of
separation.

We were pleasantly situated at this time,
and should have had no cause for unhappiness,
had not the one dark cloud been in my sky;
still all strove not to murmur, but to hope for
the best, till the worst had surely come.

CHAPTER X.

"Seest thou my home? 'tis where yon woods are waving
  In their dark richness to the sunny air;
Where yon blue stream, a thousand flower banks laving,
  Leads down the hills—a vein of light—'tis there.

Midst these green haunts how many a spring lies gleam-
      ing,
  Fring'd with the violet, color'd with the skies;
My girlhood's haunt through days of summer dreaming,
  Under young leaves that shook with melodies."
                          Felicia Hemans.

    "The loveliest village of the plain,
Where health and plenty cheered the laboring swain;
How often have I paused on every charm!
The sheltered cot, the cultivated farm,
The never-failing brook, the busy mill,
The decent church that topped the neighboring hill.
      *   *   *   *   *   *
Let the rich deride, the proud disdain
These simple blessings of the lowly train;
To me more dear, congenial to my heart,
One native charm, than all the gloss of art."
                          Oliver Goldsmith.

"My boy, thou wilt dream the world is fair,
  And thy spirit will sigh to roam;
And thou must go; but never when there
  Forget the light of home."
                          Mrs. Hale.

The Spring following our arrival in America father became acquainted with Mr. Routzahn, one of the wealthiest farmers in Frederick county. This gentleman desired that he should assist him on his farm, located three miles from the village; and as it was too far for him to return home at night, it was arranged that we should occupy a house on the place. We thought we never should like country life; still, we preferred having father with us, and were glad, under the circumstances, to make the change. The family were very social, and always cordial in their intercourse with us. Mr. and Mrs. Routzahn, a son and daughter, constituted their household group. My sisters and myself spent much of our time with Miss Routzahn, she being anxious to learn German. She was very industrious in her study of the language; indeed, in every thing else also. It might have been supposed her daily bread depended upon the accomplishment of whatever she undertook, with such zeal and persistence did she apply herself.

The modes of farming differed in some respects from those employed in Germany. The same kinds of machinery were not used. It required time to understand fully these pecu-

9

liarities; but father had been a practical farmer, and he soon overcame the difficulties in his way, and succeeded admirably. He assisted Mr. Routzahn on this farm a year; after which time it was proposed he should remove to another, still larger, five miles distant, and take full charge of it. This offer suited us in every way, and was promptly accepted. We now found ourselves most agreeably situated. It was a lovely place, and we thought there surely could be nothing more for us to desire.

This last farm was in that grouping of beautiful gardens found in Middletown valley. This valley is not unknown. It is like a diamond, more to be admired for its beauty than its size. Its population is about ten thousand souls. The inhabitants are principally farmers. Scattered here and there are many pretty villages. These are not large, but are neat and attractive, just a pleasant distance from each other. The people are industrious, and are also talkative and lively, with perhaps, if we may venture to say it, a spice of gossip, too, among them. We had reason to judge so, for we found that we as strangers, had elicited the usual amount of curiosity. When this was satisfied, we found the people kind and clever. Nor do we think

them in their interest in their neighbors' affairs
very unlike their friends and sisters who live
in towns or cities. Any new comer is a subject
of surmise, for a day at least. In large cities
there is so much to occupy one's attention, that
there is not time to be quite as curious as
villagers have the reputation of being.

I never felt like endorsing the customary
hits at village gossip, while the small talk of
older sisters, larger grown, is allowed to go
unimpeached. People will talk, whether it be
in city or in village, and the weakness is not
generally as unamiable as it is made to appear.
A village was my home all the early part of
my life; and I heard less mere idle gossip than
when I resided in a city. Fashion, parade,
show, a neighbor's style of dress, seemed to be
reigning topics, just as much as in the village,
even in an added degree in proportion to its
greater size. In either place

> " It is a custom
> More honor'd in the breach, than the observance."

There are themes lofty and ennobling, quite
enough to fill each little span of life; and it
does seem pitiable while this is true, that men
and women should condescend to the very

drudgery of speech. The evil is not often negative in its influence, but more apt always to do harm than good.

So much for our opinion of gossip, wherever found. Now I will take you, patient reader, back to Middletown valley, the beauty of which is really indescribable. It should be seen to be appreciated. Fancy a cluster of jewels: an emerald, a garnet, and an amethyst, forming a Mosaic groundwork; an atmosphere around, white and soft as a pearl, with an opal sky above; in the distance the mountains, rugged and sublime for a setting, and you see it as it appeared to me when first my eyes looked upon it, and as it has been in my memory ever since.

Mountains overlook the entire area of the valley; there they stand, God's sentinels, towering in their height, the embodiment of majesty, and fitting symbols of strength. Their sides and summits are covered with forests. They give birth to blessed streamlets, that ripple and gurgle their way to the valley below, irrigating it, and causing it to yield richly all the products of the soil. Again these streamlets form lovely brooks at the foot of the mountains, where they sparkle and spread out in silver sheen; or wearying of restraint, make a glad escape, and go laughing over pebbly beds, through fields and meadows, into farm yards, where we see them glittering and sparkling, as if in excess of joyousness.

The landscape is a network of beautiful views, a very kaleidoscope in its ever-changing scenes. Hills rise here and there, clumps of trees form natural arbors, with now and then a lonely scion of the wood, in solitary pride, lifting itself up from the earth as if scorning companionship. Under the spreading boughs cattle browse and doze the hours away, indolent and blissful, a picture of calm content.

On a graceful slope may be seen a simple village church, its gilded spire glittering in the sunlight; near it are rustic hamlets, these are picturesque, though unpretentious; scattered on the hillsides are more stylish dwellings, the homes of the wealthier residents,—the whole forming a lovely rural landscape. Truly this valley is a garden spot, abundantly fertile, lavish in its crops, in its fruits, and adorned with a luxurious growth of flowers. Well-filled barns attest how the farmer's toil has been rewarded; and there is besides a general appearance of prosperity.

Our surroundings were of a most delightful character. We almost forgot there was distress or vicissitude to be encountered. The days flew swiftly by in this Eden-home. Our parents had passed through severe perplexities, but now they looked forward to long-continued happiness. How quickly we accommodate ourselves to such a condition of things. We are ever ready to welcome joy, but are startled if sorrow follow in its wake. We are creatures easily made to laugh or weep, and hours full of happy thought are often the forerunners of those marked only by anxious foreboding.

Shortly after we were settled so comfortably in our new home, father was surprised by intelligence received in a letter from brother Andrew, that brother Charles had left his situation, and no one knew where he had gone. This distressed us all, for we supposed he was entirely satisfied with the arrangements made for him. Father and mother had not thought for a moment, even if not pleased, that he would leave without consulting them. No pains were spared to learn his whereabouts, but without avail. His plans had been so made and carried out, that all search failed. We were beginning to dread lest some dire calamity had

happened to him. We feared, at best, years
might elapse before we should hear from him.
Mother would sit for hours, wondering what
had become of her missing boy. He had started
out to bear the buffettings of the world alone.
She longed to welcome him again to her maternal care. She had tender words and loving
smiles ready to greet him when he should
return. She believed he would come back,
and patiently waited and watched;

> "For long is the time a son may roam,
>   Ere he tire his mother out."

Middletown contains six churches. The
denominations are as following: the Reformed,
the Lutheran, the Methodist, the United
Brethren, the Roman Catholic; besides these,
the colored people have a church; they are
generally Methodists in belief. The people are
religiously inclined throughout the valley, and
the various places of worship are well attended.

On Sunday morning the farmers with their
families, are seen in their carriages going to
town to worship God with the gathered multitude. After service many remain to have a
chat, while the congregation is slowly dispers-
ing. Then they return to their quiet homes.

There are three day schools in the place; these are well conducted, and the scholars make creditable improvement. I was a pupil while I remained in the village, and was much pleased with both the teachers and the scholars.

Father's business relations with Mr. Routzahn continued to be of the most pleasant character. They seemed to understand each other thoroughly. But we were destined to make another change. Miss Routzahn had married Mr. Doub, a gentleman residing in the valley, and the farm we had was desired for their home. Our friendship was unvarying, notwithstanding our separation. These were halcyon days, and they and the friends asso-. ciated with them, will always bring to us welcome remembrances.

CHAPTER XI.

"My boy, when the world is dark to thee,
Then turn to the light of home."
Mrs. Hale.

"If hearty sorrow
Be a sufficient remedy for offence,
I tender it here."
Shaks. Two Gentlemen of Verona.

"'Tis easier for the generous to forgive,
Than for offence to ask it."
Thomson's Edmund and Eleonora.

"So now is come our joyful'st feast;
Let every man be jolly;
Each room with ivy leaves is drest,
And every post with holly.
Though some churls at our mirth repine,
Round your foreheads garlands twine,
And let us all be merry."
George Wither.

Four months had elapsed since we had heard
of the disappearance of brother Charles. Father
had been unable to gain any information concerning him. We were at an utter loss to
know why he should have gone away in the

manner he had. We would not permit ourselves to cherish for a moment the idea that
any harm had overtaken him. Just when
father had determined to make no further
inquiry or search, he received a letter from my
grandfather in Germany; and strange enough,
this letter contained information relating to
Charles. He had written from Baltimore to
grandfather, and had desired that news of his
whereabouts be sent to his parents. He had
a good home with Mr. Gachle, owner of a
large piano manufactory, who had no children, and desired to adopt him. He was going
to school, and, besides, was learning music.
He longed to see father, and expressed an
earnest desire that he would come to Baltimore.
Father started immediately. On arriving at
Mr. Gachle's establishment, he inquired for
Charles. Very soon father and son met, and
great was the rejoicing. The anxiety and
suspense that had been endured were forgotten
in the happiness of the reunion.

He told father how he happened to come
to Baltimore. He had taken a fancy to the
city during the short time we were there, upon
our arrival in the country, and had determined,
if ever in his power, he would get there again.

He thought he would like to make it his home. The situation he had in Urbana did not suit him; and so on one occasion, meeting a farmer going to Baltimore with his team and produce, he seized the opportunity and accompanied the man.

It was late in the evening when they reached the city, and having neither friends nor acquaintances, he wandered desolate and lonely through the streets, wondering where he should find lodging for the night. He was sauntering along thoughtfully, and not in a very hopeful mood, when an elderly lady came up to him, and asked him why he looked so sad. He told her he had just arrived; that he was a stranger, without friends or home. She told him if he was a good boy, she could get him a home with her nephew. This was welcome intelligence, and was most gladly received. She said he must go with her to her home for the night, and the next day she would take him to her nephew's house.

After a night's rest and a good breakfast, he started with his new friend for the home she had promised him. The gentleman proved to be Mr. Gachle. He was pleased with Charles; indeed, the favorable impression was mutual, and an agreement was at once made that my brother should become one of the family. He found his friends all they appeared to be on a first acquaintance, and he was delighted with his prospects. He thought himself extremely fortunate.

Mr. and Mrs. Gaehle urged him to write to his parents, and inform them where he was. He did not tell the whole of his story, fearing it would make them think less of him. They supposed that his parents were still in Germany, and that he had come to America alone. There was an evident mystery; but he conducted himself well, and seemed to value their friendship; so his kind benefactors continued their confidence in him.

Charles hesitated writing for some time, fearing his father's displeasure; but finally he determined to write to his grandfather, explaining all the circumstances, and request him to intercede in his behalf.

During the time he had been with them, Mr. and Mrs. Gaehle had been so generous, and considerate, that he felt he could no longer withhold his full confidence. Mrs. Gaehle had been like a mother to him. He concluded to tell her all: how he had been placed at a trade by his father, but not liking his employer, he had left, and found his way to Baltimore. He told her his parents were not in Germany, but were living in Frederick county; that he had not informed his father where he was, because he believed it would sorely vex him. He said he was too unhappy to remain with the family with whom he-had been placed, therefore resolved to try and find a home for himself, and then inform his parents what he had done.

While Mrs. Gaehle sympathized with him, yet she urged him immediately to fulfil his intention of writing home, which, so far, he had failed to do. She assured him it was the only correct course. He took her advice, and wrote to grandfather, and in due time the intelligence reached father.

After hearing the flattering account of Mr. and Mrs. Gaehle, which Charles related so minutely, it could only be admitted he had indeed found true friends, and he very properly set a high value upon them. If he remained with them, they promised to educate him, and in every respect do a good part by him. Upon weighing the matter carefully, and conferring with mother, it was decided the whole occurrence was providential; and father and mother

determined not to interfere.   They gave their
consent, and Baltimore became my brother's
home.

This circumstance resulted advantageously
for Charles; yet it should be no precedent.
He should not have acted without the advice
of his parents.   Where such a course might in
one instance turn out fortunately, it is sure to
be disastrous in a majority of cases.   " Honor
thy father and mother " is the command to
which the promise is attached, " that thy days
may be long in the land which the Lord thy
God giveth thee."   The only safe plan is to
obey this command: whosoever faileth to do
so, standeth in slippery places.

Father prolonged his stay in Baltimore for a
few days after his adjustment of Charles'
affairs, to select for those at home Christmas
presents.   The season for such remembrances
had arrived, and it would not do for him to
return without taking some gift to each ex-
pectant one.   Every face would be darkened
if he came home empty-handed, and his welcome would be anything but cordial.   He knew
this, and made arrangements accordingly; for
each member of the family, down to the tiniest,
he purchased some precious love-token.

Oh, these joyous Christmas days! To the heart of a child their advent is the harbinger of joy. For the mature they also have attractions. We love to see others made happy, even though it be by the presentation of only a child's trinket. Our hearts are lighter as we look at the little ones in their Christmas frolics; and we recall the time, long past it may be, when we were children, and greeted the merry Christmas season with bounding hearts. We remember how rapturously we gazed on the heavily-laden tree; how we danced, and hopped, and skipped again in very wantonness of glee.

The heart must be cold, aye, cold unto death, that does not feel the glow of warmth shed by the brightly burning Christmas log! In the city the pleasant chimney fire is no more, but even if more modern ways be had of keeping out old King Frost, we can still in fancy bring back

"The days of yore,
When our fathers kept the Christmas time
And burned the Yule that is no more.

When walls of hall and hut were hung
With ivy and with holly boughs;
And minstrels went from house to house,
And all night long their carols sung.

When jolly dancers shook the floor
With country reels, which fiddlers played;

And many a little man and maid
At blind-man's buff and battle door,

Peopled the corners with delight;
The old folks sat at fox-and-goose,
And let their tongues and fancies loose
In tales of lords and ladies bright.

And then the world of solid cheer,
In meats and drinks for rich and poor;
The meanest kept an open door,
For Christmas came but once a year."

Father returned, bringing his treasures, and we hailed him with glad huzzas. Our gifts were stowed snugly away, we were not even permitted to see the contents of the mysterious packages; but we feasted our imagination on what they might contain. We listened eagerly to father's account of Charles and his new home. We thought his adventures had been marvellous, and we wondered if he would have as good a time as we knew we should when Christmas came.

When the day arrived, and we all were assembled to eat the Christmas dinner, we missed our absent brother; but we knew he had found friends, and our only regret was that he could not be with us to share our mirth and feasting. We wanted him to help us to welcome the advent of old Santa Claus, the patron saint of all good children everywhere.

When evening had closed in, and the lamps were lit, we gathered round our well-filled bush, and to each were given the pretty things that had been placed there for them by loving hands. Again we missed our brother. Thus it is at all times, joy with regret is blended. From our family chain one link was missing, and the thought would come back to us in our gayest hours. Yet we were happy, though a single pleasure was withheld. We had no sympathy with those who in dismal tones would croak,

> "The merry Christmas days are past,
> The antique plenty is no more."

Our heart was with "the living present;" and, ever when the rolling seasons should bring round the joyous Christmas time, we hoped to

> "Feast until the tapers shine
> And day is dead and curfews toll."

CHAPTER XII.

"One sorrow which throws
Its bleak shade alike o'er our joys and our woes;
To which life nothing darker or brighter can bring,
For which joy has no balm and affliction no sting!"
Moore.

"Oh, how this spring of life resembleth
The uncertain glory of an April day,
Which now shows all the beauty of the sun,
And, by-and-by, a cloud takes all away!"
Shakspeare.

"What can we not endure,
When pains are lessened by the hope of cure?"
Nabb's Microcosmus.

"How disappointment tracks
The steps of hope!"
Miss Landon.

"Who finds not Providence all good and wise,
Alike in what it gives, and what denies?"
Pope's Essay on Man.

The cloud that for a long time had been darkening my sky, was now fast shutting the sunlight out forever. My sight was rapidly failing. I could scarcely see well enough to distinguish objects. Deep shadows were gathering over everything in Nature. I felt that it was my doom to sit in perpetual darkness. Physicians all agreed in the opinion that my sight could not be restored, and the unwelcome intelligence bore heavily upon my spirits, already much depressed by the overhanging dread I had for months endured. I strove to bear with resignation the fearful affliction now so surely in store for me. The dispensation seemed severe, yet I tried not to murmur. I felt as if life would be only a period of suffering. The outer world was being hid from me, yet God had sent this great sorrow to me. He knew its uses; I must wait to know.

Notwithstanding the cause I had for being sad, and my family, in sympathy with me, yet we all were happy in every other respect. Peace and plenty were the presiding angels of our homestead. There was but the one sorrow to mar our felicity. Our hearts would doubtless be too surely wedded to earth, too closely knit to its fleeting joys, were it not that ever there is something to call our thoughts away from things of time and sense; something to make us look forward to a home where bliss alone doth reign; where no sorrow nor pain cometh.

Oh, weary hearts, rejoice, "earth has no sorrow which heaven cannot cure." Oh, delvers in earth's alloy, be of good cheer, in heaven the very streets are paved with "pure gold like unto clear glass." Oh, ye who sit in darkness with folded hands and pensive brow, lift up your songs of everlasting praise. In yon city of the New Jerusalem, ye have no need of sun, or moon, or golden candlestick, for there is no night there. And ye may look upon the King in all His beauty, throned in majesty, and ye may see Him as He is. There will be no dimmed vision, no orbs obscured; but clearer sight than was ever vouchsafed on earth shall be given, with which to gaze through all eternity upon glory ineffable, and the faces of the loved lost for a time to earthly contemplation.

Father used every means to improve the condition of my eyes. A number of physicians had been consulted, but with no encouragement that a healthy restoration could be hoped for. It was thought by some, perhaps, I might retain imperfect vision for years, provided I did not tax my sight by reading or study.

I had been under careful medical treatment for two years, but without improvement.

When a very little girl, a slight humor had appeared on my head, of this I had been relieved, but the disease had settled in my eyes and was the cause of my eventual loss of sight. One day a stranger who had been overtaken by a storm, took shelter in our house. He observed the inflamed appearance of my eyes, and inquired of father the cause. Father explained to him the symptoms that had from time to time been developed, and he also told the visitor he feared a total loss of sight was inevitable. Our guest thought not so; he said he knew a remedy which could not fail to arrest the inflammation; then the eyes would be entirely well again. This was, indeed, joyful intelligence; and as every previous remedy had failed, we hoped this might be successful. It was to apply red precipitate, a poisonous preparation of mercury, mixed with unsalted butter, to my eyes. It was done as the stranger had said it should be, three times a day. The result was most disastrous; the calamity of my life was hastened. I refer to this circumstance that persons may avoid the use, especially under conditions of so serious a character as those peculiar to my case, of any mere quack prescription. While the aid of

skilful physicians can be secured, the foolish
advice of ignorant men and women should not
be listened to.

Very soon after the application of the precipitate, I found I could not distinguish objects,
could only tell day from night. I do not mean
to say that my loss of sight was occasioned by
following this man's advice, for it had been
decided to be inevitable; but all who knew of
its use, believed the evil had been hastened.
If the outer world were to become a blank to
me, the more precious every moment of sight.
This can only be appreciated by those who
have suffered.

When it became a fact that nothing could
be done for me, my father and mother, brothers
and sisters, strove to make home the more
cheerful. They tried to lessen, if they could,
not scatter the gloom. We spent many happy
hours even at this period, though they moved
hand in hand with sorrow. My sisters and I
attended Sunday school near by, located in the
woods. It has been truly said,

"The groves were God's first temples, ere man had
        learned
  To hew the shaft and lay the architrave,
  And spread the roof above them; ere he framed
  The lofty vault, to gather and roll back

The sound of anthems; in darkling wood,
Amidst the cool and silence, he knelt down,
And offered to the Mightiest solemn thanks
And supplication."

This quiet little church, hid away in the forest, seemed the very place to worship. "The proud old world beyond" was shut out, and the song of praise or voice of prayer was interrupted only by the sweet melody of bird, gently purling rivulet, or rustling leaves, as stirred by some breeze they mingled in the anthem, swelling from hearts attuned by the harmonies of this woodland sanctuary. Surely simplicity finds readiest acceptance in the eyes of Him who was all meekness and humility, and who divested Himself of His kingly glory and became man, that man through Him might regain the image of his Maker so sadly scarred by sin.

I have often dwelt with tender memory upon my visits to this forest church, with its rural architecture; its hard, uncushioned benches, with their high straight backs; its plain pulpit, with no gallery for its choir, and no organ to make vocal the woods around; and though I have heard sweeter music, more majestic symphonies, I have never heard hymns sung in more sincere accord with the pious thought expressed. We build our churches great and grand, emblems they may be

> "Of boundless power
> And inaccessible majesty."

This may be well in cities full, in an age of progress; but if these lofty fanes, with sculptured domes or sky kissing spires, lead for an instant the wayward heart from teachings it should cherish, they are nought. Better kneel by the roadside or on Sahara's sands and offer supplication, than worship with the outward form, while the senses are betrayed by any external loveliness from that inner court where God himself doth reign.

> Thou dear rustic Church of my youth
> Where were gathered lessons of truth,
> Long shall be cherished thy form as of yore,
> Thy ungarnished walls and dark oaken door.
>
> When weary of show I turn to thee now,
> And sincerely renew youth's early vow;
> In fancy again there fall on my ear
> The tones of some loved one in prayer.
>
> A memory sweet of the vanishing past,
> Thou art to me, too lovely to last;
> And each leaflet that remindeth of thee,
> I treasure with my heart's deep sanctity.

As Miss Routzahn's marriage had indirectly influenced my father's business prospects, he concluded to carry out a plan he had for some time been considering; he wished to purchase a medium sized property and settle on it permanently. It was further his intention it should have grounds sufficiently extensive to admit his having a fruit and vegetable garden, as he intended to cultivate these for the Frederick market.

He had not felt that he could honorably close his engagement with Mr. Routzahn; now the turn affairs had taken, enabled him to execute his long-cherished purpose. He succeeded in purchasing a suitable place; but the enterprize failed. He found the market overstocked, and could not secure sale for his produce. He disposed of his property, and removed again to the village of Middletown. He here secured a situation in Mr. Schlosser's tannery. This enabled us to live comfortably, but with strict economy.

Our home was not, of course, so pleasant as when we were on the farm; but we had cheerful hearts and willing hands, and readily accommodated ourselves to our new mode of living. We had thought, on our first removal

11

to the country, we should never become accustomed to it. We had always resided in a village, and supposed we should miss the excitement of such life; but we had been agreeably disappointed, and now felt sorry to leave the woods and fields, with all the accompaniments of rustic living. We should, however, still hear the song of birds, the low of cattle, and even the peculiar intonation of the frogs, at eventide; noisy, truly, but still a sort of fantastic music of their own, a contralto, it may have been, deepening sometimes into heavy basso. We were glad of this, for we had learned to enjoy every description of rural pleasure.

In leaving our woodland home, we should have to give up many of its characteristic recreations and employments; yet we did not intend to repine. We had been taught to make the best of everything, and when a change of circumstances occurred beyond our control, to believe all was for our good; to take courage from the wholesome teaching—

"When thy best is fully done,
    Welcome what thou canst not shun."

So we accepted our lot without a murmur,

knowing that, although we would not have planned it thus, had we had it in our power to adjust events, yet a kind Father held us as the waters in the hollow of His hand," and would appoint all things wisely.

Resignation is a lesson we must learn well, for we shall need the grace in each day's experience. Sacrifice is a part of every life, indeed, enters into every moment. If there be one principle more evident than another in any character, that has attained eminence for its real excellence in the full sense of the term, it is that of subduing selfish aims; and while enjoying what is felicitous, enduring what may seem unpropitious, meekly.

With the certain prospect of the constant need of this spirit of self-abnegation, would it not be well for us to strive, by living example, to reconcile those by whom we are surrounded to its willing acceptance? It will save many a heartache, and many a bitter struggle, that otherwise might be made, calmly to abide issues beyond our control.

CHAPTER XIII.

"Seasons return, but not to me returns
Day, or the sweet approach of e'en or morn,
Or light of vernal bloom, or Summer's rose,
Or flocks, or herds, or human face divine;
But clouds instead, and ever during dark
Surrounds me, from the cheerful ways of men
Cut off, and for the Book of knowledge fair
Presented with an universal blank."

John Milton.

"Perfumes, the more they're chaf'd, the more they render
Their pleasant scents; and so affliction
Expresseth virtue fully, whether true
Or else adulterate."

John Webster.

"The path of sorrow, and that path alone,
Leads to the land where sorrow is unknown;
No traveller ever reach'd that blest abode,
Who found not thorns and briars in his road."

Cowper.

The remainder of my simple story will be
from a blind girl's pen. I will not harrow the
feelings of my kind and sympathetic reader
with an attempt to tell how heavily on my
heart fell the sad truth that I was blind. God
had been very good, and would be still. I

could trust Him, although my way henceforth would be utter darkness, yet He would lead me, and my feet would not slide. I could now plead from my very soul, with the fervid eloquence of one who had known the same struggles with the same mournful result,

"So much the rather thou, celestial Light,
  Shine inward, and the mind through all her powers
  Irradiate, there plant eyes; all mist from thence
  Purge and disperse, that I may see and tell
  Of things invisible to mortal sight."

I had been fortunate above a number, for the priceless boon of sight had been mine during the first twelve years of my life. I had remembrance to aid me. I had seen Nature in her forms of beauty; had looked upon the human face divine ; and now in the years to come, should at least be able mentally to see these again.

I have since learned that the blind have modes of communicating with the outer world, through the intensifying of the other senses. In this way they really enjoy life, and, as a class, they may be considered a happy people. They are known to participate in common recreations, such as leap-frog, touch, hoop-bowling, skipping with a rope, shuttlecock, marbles, etc., and even the sports of sliding and snowballing.

We are told of a certain John Metcalf, who pursued numerous avocations without much hindrance from the loss of sight. As a boy, he went birds'-nesting with his schoolmates; as a young man, he followed the hounds, he learnt to swim and to dive, had the reputation of being a good boxer, was a good musician, dealt in woollen goods, and also in horses, established public conveyances, became a builder and contractor, built bridges, laid down roads, made drains, and accomplished some difficult engineering works which people who had their sight declined. This versatility of talent is, of course, rare, combined, as it must have been, with indomitable energy and perseverance. Still, it goes to prove that blindness need not prevent the development of mental or physical activity.

Then, too, there are interesting accounts of the use of what are termed the unrecognized senses, which greatly facilitate the communication of the blind with external objects. Facial perception is remarkable as one of these. We are told of a Mr. Levy, who, whether within a house or in the open air, whether walking or standing still, could tell, although quite blind, when he was opposite an object, and could perceive whether it were tall or short, slender or bulky. He could detect whether it were a solitary object or a continuous fence; whether it were a close fence or composed of open rails, and often whether a wooden fence, a brick or stone wall, or a quick-set hedge. It is said these objects were perceived through the skin of the face, and the impressions were immediately transmitted to the brain. Stopping the ears did not interfere with this power, so the currents of air could have nothing to do with it, but covering the face with a thick veil would destroy it altogether. None of the five senses had anything to do with it; hence it has been termed facial perception.

There are many curious illustrations of this faculty recorded; such as being able to distinguish shops from private houses; even to point out doors and windows, and this whether the doors be shut or open ; to detect when the lower part of a fence is brickwork and the upper part rails, and to perceive the line where the two meet ; to discover irregularities in height and projections, and indentations in walls. There is a curious story related in confirmation of this faculty. Mr. Levy, himself blind from earliest infancy, Director of the Association for Promoting the General Welfare of the Blind, and a resident of London, England, narrates the following: " While walking with a friend in Forest Lane, Stratford, I said, pointing to a fence which separated the road from a field, 'those rails are not quite as high as my shoulder.' He looked at them and said they were higher. We, however, measured, and found them about three inches lower than my shoulder. At the time of making this observation, I was about four feet from the rails." Certainly in this instance facial perception was more accurate than sight.

A similar sense belongs to some part of the animal creation, and especially to bats, who have been known to fly about a room without striking against anything after the cruel experiment has been made of extracting their eyes. These, and similar interesting facts, are to be found in a well-known work, " Blindness and the Blind, or a treatise on the Science of Typhology." By W. Hanks Levy, F. R. G. S., London.

Many persons entertain erroneous ideas concerning the blind. They seem to regard them as unlike other people, a separate and distinct class in all their susceptibilities and endowments. They speak of them as incapacitated for many pursuits. From some they may be debarred, it is true, but their resources and abilities are far more numerous than the unreflective might suppose. Still in their helplessness in many respects, they appeal strongly to those more fortunate than themselves, and while to be regarded with pity is extremely galling, a tender consideration is always grateful to them.

What may be done for the blind is a subject of very much more importance than the general public may understand it to be. But the humane everywhere have joined hands to alleviate suffering in this form; while the thoughtful and judgmatic are endeavoring to solve this problem so pregnant with good or ill to those whose misfortune it is to be blind; and strenuous efforts are being made to mitigate, in some degree, the dreadful calamity of having "wisdom at one entrance quite shut out," and that the most important entrance.

In England, France and America, the interest is rapidly on the increase, and much careful thought is being devoted to the matter. And from the worn artisan, whose sight, too severely taxed, has faded out; from the victim of pestilence; from the sufferer from accident; aye, and from the babe, whose heritage has been a soul shut within the body's portals, is arising one united voice of thankfulness to those who have espoused their cause. God will lend a helping hand. He will bless and crown with full success all such heaven-directed effort.

CHAPTER XIV.

"Great minds, like heaven, are pleased
In doing good."
Rowe's Tamerlane.

"In faith and hope the world will disagree,
But all mankind's concern is charity:
All must be false that thwart this one great end;
And all of God, that bless mankind, or mend."
Pope's Essay on Man.

"Thus bravely live heroic men,
A consecrated band;
Life is to them a battle-field,
Their hearts a holy land."
Tuckerman.

"'Tis not in mortals to command success;
But we'll do more, Sempronius, we'll deserve it."
Addison's Cato.

Far more interest has been shown of late years in the education of the blind than in the past, and noble men and women have addressed themselves earnestly to labor in their behalf. Institutions are multiplying, and are successful beyond expectation, in the good they are accomplishing. Ways and means to facilitate the communication of knowledge are being carefully studied.

Buildings, spacious in themselves, and surrounded by extensive pleasure grounds, are now appropriated.

The mental and physical development of this class of persons has become one of the benevolences of the day. And no more magnanimous enterprise could be offered the humanitarian than such a field of labor. Citizens of large heart and noble sympathies are actively engaged in the good work, and the processes for assisting the blind are now so thorough, that they enjoy facilities for obtaining easy access to the resources of literature, music, and to any of the mechanical arts for which they have capacity; indeed, almost every branch of industry is now within their reach. All are afforded opportunities to obtain a thoroughly scholastic education, and, so far, efforts made to instruct them have proved that talent, in creditable ratio, is found among them. This movement is of more recent date in America than Europe, and has not reached the advanced ground here that it has there. Still, the work is progressing.

There are numerous examples of rare and exceptional talent among the blind; nor is the larger endowment that of genius without a goodly number of representatives. With the acknowledged types of these two classes may be identified the distinguished blind philologist, Scapinelli, one of the most accomplished scholars of his day; Count de Pagan, who, on becoming blind, devoted himself to the study of fortification and geometry; Dr. Nicholas Saunderson, who, although blind almost from his birth, lectured upon optics, and was professor of mathematics in the University of Cambridge; Sir John Fielding, half-brother of the great novelist, and Chief Magistrate of Bow Street Police Court, whose " acuteness on the magisterial bench may have been equalled, but has never been surpassed;" Huber, the eminent naturalist, who invented the glass bee-hives now in common use; nor have these examples of scholarly excellence and practical adaptability of the same been without a peer in heroism and indomitable will-power, as shown by one James Holman, who travelled without an attendant through a large portion of Europe, penetrated five thousand miles into the Russian dominions, performed a voyage round the world, and actually, on one occasion, saved the vessel by taking the helm.

These illustrations are somewhat removed,

we admit; but we are not without promising indications of talent and usefulness of no ordinary type in America. Time will show creditable results compared with any that have been cited. Students in the Institutions in this country have, upon the completion of the required course of preparation, been admitted to the bar, as was instanced in the case of James B. Green, a pupil of the Baltimore Institution, and later a graduate of the University of Virginia, a gentleman whose fine literary acumen is unmistakeable, and whose commencement thesis, with "Milton" for its subject, was forceful in style, and of positive æsthetic excellence.

Poetry has been aspired to in no ordinary sense by Morrison Heady, of Kentucky, whose productions have a classic ring in them, and suggest the thought, the lyre has been touched by a hand so skilful, that time may prove the poet to have been in his earlier efforts a master of the art divine, in embryo, whose bolder flights had placed him on Parnassian heights.

The pulpit has not been without representatives from among the blind. We read of an eloquent old man in the far West, Paul Denver, who held ·enchained unnumbered hosts he

never looked upon; his long white hair swaying to the breeze, his whole face beaming with
emotion, and tears reigning from his sightless
eyes, as he plead with perishing men to flee
from the wrath to come, and find redemption
in His blood who died on the cross for them.
Nearer home, and of more recent distinction,
is William Henry Milburn, who has, perhaps,
no superior in oratorical finish and fervid
eloquence. As a lecturer, also, he has attained
marked celebrity. His travels abroad have
furnished varied and interesting incident for
these.

I had frequently heard of Institutions for
the education of the blind, and when the last
hope for the recovery of my sight, even par-
tially, had faded, I began to feel an earnest
desire to secure admission into one of these.
My love for knowledge was great, and besides,
it was necessary for me to think of some way
in which I could earn a livelihood; for my
father had met with reverses, and could not do
much for me. Then, too, the probability was
I should outlive my parents, as my health was
good, and I was still very young. I could not
bear to think of being dependent upon the
bounty of others, therefore I was the more

desirous to prepare myself in some way to make a livelihood.

There were serious obstacles before me, my parents' means being limited. I supposed it would be attended with great expense to gain admission into such Institution, and had almost ceased to hope for the consummation of my wishes. My great need, however, made me still cling to the possibility, faint though it appeared.

About this time the pupils of the Baltimore Institution for the Blind gave a concert in Frederick. I attended, and was delighted with the music. Both the vocal and instrumental performances were excellent. I now determined to make every effort I could to become a pupil. I craved an education, for I knew without it I could never be self-dependent, and this was my chief ambition. Two gentlemen, Mr. Cole and Mr. Stoner, had, from time to time, expressed great interest in me, also willingness to aid me, if in their power. I spoke to these friends and asked them to counsel me as to the plan by which I should proceed to arrive at some understanding of the conditions under which I could be admitted. Mr. Cole wrote to Mr. Keener, who was at that time Superintend-

ent of the Institution. He laid my case before
this gentleman, and urged that my wish be
considered favorably. Mr. Stoner had been a
resident of Middletown but a short time. He
had contracted for the building of a church,
and while this was being erected, he made the
place his home. He paid frequent business
visits to Baltimore. On one of these occasions
he called at the Institution and had an interview with Mr. Keener, who spared no pains in
informing him of the manner in which the
blind were taught, and showed him all the
needed appliances, the various systems of teaching employed, the style of printing, and many
other interesting features of the Institution.
He was very courteous and affable, and the
account of this interview increased my desire
to accomplish my long-cherished purpose.

During a second visit to the Institution, Mr.
Stoner was introduced to a lady, Miss Mary L.
Day, who was being educated there, and who
spoke in the warmest terms of everything connected with the place. She had at this time with
the aid of friends prepared her biography, and
was finding for it ready sale. The book was
entitled "Incidents in the Life of a Blind Girl."
She very kindly sent me a copy, and I found

12

it pleasant and entertaining. The story was a simple one, yet full of interest; and by its sale Miss Day has realized a moderate competency.

The charitable and kindly disposed everywhere would be likely to encourage such an effort. A life-history may be very plain, perhaps uneventful, in the usual acceptation of the term, but if it has been blighted by a great sorrow, there will always be found those whose hearts will go out towards the stricken one, and practical sympathy will not be withheld. How forcible the teaching of Paul, in his letter to the Corinthians, "Though I speak with the tongues of men and of angels and have not charity, I am become as sounding brass or a tinkling cymbal;" and yet again he dwells upon the theme—"Now abideth faith, hope, charity, these three: but the greatest of these is charity."

This shows the Apostle's high estimate of this principle of love in its full sense, and what a cardinal virtue he deemed it in a Christ-like character. It is an ornament more to be desired than jewels or costly apparel. Golconda's rarest germ is naught compared with it. Gold of Ophir, studded with liquid diamonds, pales before it. Pearls from the depth of the sea, though gracing a coronet, are less pure than its dewy light. No words are eloquent enougn to express its true beauty; yet we may wear it, a gift from Him who is all charity, as He is love:

> "True charity, a plant divinely nurs'd,
>   Fed by the love from which it rose at first,
>   Thrives against hope, and in the rudest scene,
>   Storms but enliven its unfading green;
>   Exuberant is the shadow it supplies,
>   Its fruit on earth, its growth above the skies."

Beside the book, Miss Day sent me a oead basket she had made. It was ingeniously contrived—was very pretty and tasty. These gifts added to my previous desire to share instructions and opportunities of every kind extended to those similarly situated with myself. I thought if I only knew how to manipulate vari-colored beads as Miss Day had done I should be glad, and could, perhaps, make it a source of revenue.

To writing a book I did not then aspire; but Providence opened the way for me, and in good time I enjoyed the privileges I had so longed for.

CHAPTER XV.

"Just as a mother, with sweet pious face,
  Yearns tow'rds her children from her seat,
Gives one a kiss, another an embrace,
  Takes this upon her knee, that on her feet;
And while from actions, looks, complaints, pretences,
  She learns their feelings and their various will:
To this a look, to that a word dispenses,
  And whether stern or smiling, loves them still,
So Providence helps all our wants,
And what is best at all times grants."

Anon.

"Now ye stand
Eager to spring upon the promised land,
Fair ye see triumph, pleasure, fame and joy:
Friendship unwavering, love without alloy,
Brave thoughts of noble deeds and glory won,
Like angels, beckon ye to venture on."

Frances Kemble Butler.

My hope was strong, and I could not help anticipating a favorable result to my wishes; although, as yet, there had been no very promising indications. I believed I should secure admission to the Institution, by what means or through what influence I could not foresee. I knew my friends were zealous, and would leave no resource untried that might terminate fortunately.

I had been taught "faith is the substance of things hoped for, the evidence of things not seen," and now I had proof of this lesson of trust. Mr. Cole received an answer to the letter he had written Mr. Keener, stating that application had been made to the Governor of the State, and he had granted the privilege, and had furnished the necessary legal document upon which I was to become a pupil in the Institution. It was thought I had best enter at once, as all arrangements had been made.

I was greatly rejoiced at my good fortune, and very thankful to those who had aided me in securing it. It seemed as if a new, bright future had suddenly opened before me. Fancy was at once busily engaged picturing my changed circumstances, the opportunity I should have for improvement; the delightful intercourse with those, like myself, deprived of sight, and how I should gain strength hearing of their victories. My affliction had made me thoughtful beyond my years, and I weighed the matter well. Heart and brain were full to overflowing, but I did not forget that my Heavenly Father had bestowed this great blessing upon his sightless child.

Several ladies in our village assisted mother in getting me ready for school. They were busy for a few days refitting my wardrobe, and seemed so glad and happy that I was going. The surly misanthrope may talk of selfishness being dominant in the heart of man, and may strive to make any, who will listen to his miserable croakings, believe that true, disinterested friendship is only a name; but he will not succeed, save with churls like himself, for there are too many evidences to the contrary, broad cast o'er the earth. All around us are the generous and the true who love to do a kindly turn for friendship's sake alone, with no slightest tinge of sordid motive lurking in any hidden corner of the heart. Not with a passive kindliness are they content, but seek active means of proving their good will. It is not enough that we wish well to others. Our feelings should clothe themselves with corresponding actions. The spring which has no outlet becomes a stagnant pool, while that which pours itself off in the running stream is pure and living, and is the cause of life and beauty wherever it flows.

Thanks to the assistance of our village friends, I was soon ready. The day for leaving home

arrived; the hour of parting brought its struggle; it was different from anything I had
known. I had never left my father and mother
to remain away any length of time. My
mother had been so watchful over me, I did
not know what I should do without her care.
From my brothers and sisters I felt loth to go,
and when the moment came, a sensation of
dread stole over me lest we should never meet
again. We all experienced a degree of fear
that we were separating, never more to be an
undivided family. We strove to shake this
foreboding off, to regard the event as one altogether propitious, and to believe that our
family group would again be formed, with each
of us in the accustomed place.

Though we had some sad thoughts, yet father,
mother, sisters and brothers, were happy that
I was going where I should be able to garner
stores of knowledge, which would make less
solitary my darkened path. Mother would
doubtless silently grieve that in my helplessness
she could not be near her stricken child. How
precious this

> "Mother-love, unchilled by change,
> Absence wide, and coldness strange,
> Mother-love that here must yearn
> In vain for its full return."

I knew in leaving home my name would still be a household word; and I, when only strangers were round me, could wander back, and by the spirit's power steal into their midst, lay my hand in theirs, take the vacant chair beside them, could again bask in a sister's smile, felt if not seen, and fold myself confidingly away in

"Sister-love, so calm and so wise,
　Starlight risen on darkened skies."

Memory would bring them to me at eventide, at the matin-hour, at noon's high flush, and when sable night had settled on the earth, and on bended knee I could ask "Our Father" to hold in tender keeping my loved and distant ones. I could pray that He who put on humanity's garb and knew every heart-throb of sorrow would shield them from all harm:

"O, the precious privilege
　To the absent given,
Sending by the dove of prayer
　Loving words to heaven!
Arrows from the burning sun
　Cleave the quivering air,
Swifter, softlier, surer on
　Speeds the dove of prayer,
Bearing from the parted lips
　Words of tend'rest love,
Warm, as from the heart they gush'd
　To the throne above!"

Very precious are these home affections; earth would be a dreary waste without them. Our hearts would be desolate, did they not feel other hearts had need of them.

"None may name a drearier thought,
  Hearts we lean on need us not.
  If they ask for us no more,
  Gathering in heaven's affluent store,
  Life is lonelier than we knew,
  Sharper anguish thrills death through:
  In this rubbish-heap of earth
  Hides no pearl heaven's saving worth."

Our souls may wing their flight through illimitable space, and nestle at home. This makes the poignancy of separation less, and we can smile through our tears as the bright sun of an April day looks through raindrops, setting forth the truth that our lives are two-fold in their kind.

After a few hours' travel, father and I arrived in Baltimore. As it was early in the day, we went immediately to the Institution. We were cordially received by the Superintendent. He greeted me as a member of his family, this made me feel at home. We first visited the girl's department. All welcomed me kindly, and expressed great pleasure that I was to be one of their number. I felt that I should be

13

contented and happy with such warm-hearted associates. I was next introduced to Miss Bond, the matron of the Institution. This lady had such a pleasant address, was so winning in manner, that I was attracted to her, and was impressed we should be excellent friends.

I knew I should love my home; everything was so bright and cheerful; and time proved my conclusion correct in every particular.

A concert took place in the evening. Father remained, and had an opportunity of hearing some good music, which I also enjoyed greatly. The attendance was large, and everybody appeared well entertained. The laughing chorus gave the most pleasure, judging from the applause with which it was received. You would scarcely have thought blind people could have been as excessively merry as the hearty laughter in this song made them appear. The mirth was contagious, and the guests joined in chorus with the performers.

For the blind there is, perhaps, no greater enjoyment than that afforded by the harmony of sweet sounds. It is to them a language full of sentiment. They discover great aptitude in learning music. It becomes, in many instances, a mode of earning a comfortable living. This being the case, the art receives much attention in all institutions for the education of this class. A generous proportion of time is devoted to piano instruction, and due regard is also paid to the violin and flute. Concerts are given weekly, and the pupils succeed in making them very interesting to visitors.

Exhibitions of their skill, before the Legislature, have appealed strongly to the sympathies of that body, and aid has been secured in the form of liberal appropriations for the general advancement of the pupils.

Father delayed a few days in the city, in order to cheer and encourage me if I should become home-sick. But I had already found friends, and did not feel that those by whom I was surrounded were, a short time before, strangers. I seemed to have known and loved them a long while. He was delighted to see me so satisfied, and bade me good-bye less reluctantly than he would have done if I had been unwilling to be left.

He charged me to be diligent in all my studies, but to pay especial attention to my music. We then parted; a momentary sadness stole over our hearts, but it was only a passing cloud, behind which the sun was brightly shining. My home promised well, and it was best I should be separated from those very dear to me for awhile.

CHAPTER XVI.

"I go to seek my own hearth-stone
Bosomed in yon green hills alone;
A simple lodge in a pleasant land,
Whose groves the frolic fairies planned,
Where arches green the livelong day
Echo the blackbird's roundelay,"
Ralph Waldo Emerson.

"There's beauty all around our paths, if but our watchful eyes
Can trace it midst familiar things, and through their
lowly guise,
We may find it where a hedge-row showers its blossoms o'er our way,
Or a cottage window sparkles forth in the last red
light of day.

Yes, beauty dwells in all our paths, but sorrow, too,
is there;
How oft some cloud within us dims the bright still
summer air!
And yet 'tis by the lights and clouds through which
our pathway lies,
By the beauty and the grief alike we are training for
the skies."
Felicia Hemans.

Almost a century since, prompted by the
solicitations of a benevolent lady who employed

her whole life in efforts to alleviate the wants of the blind, M. Hany made an appeal to his countrymen, which resulted in the establishment of one of the largest institutions for the blind in Europe.

This gentleman invented a method of printing books for the use of the blind in embossed characters. The paper, when properly prepared, was laid upon the type, which had been previously set upon a frame for the purpose. A pressure was then made upon the paper, which gave the letters in relief on the opposite side. These letters could be distinguished by the touch with almost as much precision as those printed in the ordinary method can be perceived by the eye. Books prepared in this way had but one inconvenience—that of their extreme bulk. Subsequent improvements, however, have considerably reduced their size. And though a given amount of matter occupies a much larger surface of paper, and one volume printed in the common way makes two or three when prepared for the blind, still when we consider the benefits that flow from an invention displaying so much skill and benevolence, such a defect is of trifling importance.

The more difficult task of teaching the blind

to write is accomplished by simple contrivances. The writing board is formed by pasting on a piece of paste board of the size of a common sheet of paper, strips of the same material, forming parallel lines about half an inch from each other. This board is placed under the paper, and the finger is then drawn along upon the surface, so as to press it in the grooves or between the lines. The pupil is then taught to form the letters with a common lead pencil. After writing a word, he measures with the forefinger of the left hand the space to be left between the words. Thus by this simple process is gained for the blind all the advantages that are conferred upon seeing persons by the ruled paper.

The apparatus employed in the study of arithmetic is simple and effective. It consists of a slab of brass, cast in such a manner as to be divided into some hundreds of holes; into these holes are inserted types representing the same figures that are used by seeing persons. In this way the blind student is enabled to cipher with as much facility as a seeing one.

The study of geography is pursued by the aid of maps and globes adapted to the touch. The maps are made of wood, with indentations representing rivers, lakes, gulfs, bays, channels, &c. The mountains are designated by being rough and slightly raised, and the boundary lines of States, the principal cities and towns, are marked by pin heads, the pins being driven into the map.

In this age of progress these various plans are being constanly improved upon and many obstacles are being removed from the thorough education and development of the blind.

A joint committee from the General Assembly of Maryland visited the Institution, located on Saratoga street, the property formerly owned by Mr. König. A thorough examination was made of the various departments, and each received much commendation. In their report they recommended an appropriation to aid in procuring more suitable buildings for the further prosecution of the philanthropic plan. In order to give the Legislature an opportunity of judging more correctly of the merits of the blind, the pupils soon after visited Annapolis and gave a concert in the Legislative Hall.

Some ten years previous it had been proposed establishing an Institution for the education of the blind of the State. The plan was to

create a fund for the purpose before referred
to, and after strenuous effort the accomplishment of the proud design was effected. Through
the praiseworthy action of the Legislature at
that time, by which that Honorable Body appropriated the handsome sum of fifty thousand
dollars, and the appropriation of ten thousand
dollars by the City Council of the previous
year, in addition to the funds already accu-
mulated, those interested were enabled to com-
mence plans on such an improved and liberal
scale as must meet the wants of the State for
many years to come.

The structure erected on Boundary Avenue
is the result of this effort, and is at once a
credit to the State and an ornament to the
city. Its comforts are as ample as its accommodations. It is healthy and commanding in
location, and is, in every respect, a worthy
expression of the philanthropy of Baltimoreans.

This beautiful home was received by the
blind with feelings of the deepest gratitude
and humble thanks to Almighty God who had
put it into the hearts of the people to carry out
so good and great a work.

During the first years of my stay in Baltimore, brother Charles was still there. He was

in the cigar business, and was succeeding beyond his expectations. Mr. Gaehle had been unfortunate in business, had failed, and shortly afterwards had died. Mrs. Gaehle had gone West. How many and what unlooked-for changes cross our paths. We lay plans for future fulfilment, and lo! when the future has become the present, they are nought. It is fitly said, " Man proposes, God disposes." And we have the thought in another form from Shakspeare's pungent pen :

"There is a divinity that shapes our ends,
Rough hew them as we will."

Whatever our aims may be, they are ever overruled by One, who in His omniscience, knows the end from the beginning. The unthinking call it destiny, and tell us we are but toys in the fickle goddess' hands; but it is a higher power that governs all. He moulds our lives as He wills. How vain our murmuring, even in the little things of life, the sparrow's fall, the bending blade of grass fanned by an infant's breath—God is in all and over all.

Charles had looked forward to a long-continued relationship with his friend and benefactor; but it was otherwise ordained, and

doubtless wisely so, though to him inscrutable.
What a lesson may be learned when we see a
prosperous man, one upright in his daily walk,
suddenly stricken by death! The warning is
being constantly afforded us, but in the hurry
of the hour we too often pause not to consider.

My brother frequently called on me at the
Institution, and this made it seem even more
homelike. I had been at school about six
weeks when the vacation came round. Charles
took me home to spend the Summer months
with our family. This was very pleasant. The
prospect had lessened the pain of separation,
and with bounding heart I hastened to my
mother's side, that I might narrate my many
experiences since last at home. All were glad
to greet us, and our return was celebrated with
great rejoicing.

It is a trite expression, the form of which is
almost worn out, "there is no place like home;"
but the poet, himself homeless, was "faithful
and far-seeing" in so simply expressing the
touching sentiment. Hearts have throbbed
with renewed life at the eloquent syllables, and
eyes have moistened while lips tremblingly
repeated them.

"There blend the ties that strengthen
   Our hearts in hours of grief,
The silver links that lengthen
   Joy's visits when most brief."

Man may wander the whole earth o'er; may find his way through the swamps and jungles of distant Africa; may cool his fevered brow in the waters of the open polar sea; or lave his limbs in limpid waves, 'neath a Southern sky; he may greet the sun as he looks forth in morning light, or track him to his nightly couch behind the gold-fringed curtains of the West; yet his wanderings o'er, the spot where his mother first sung a lullaby to soothe him to sleep,—even the cradle in which he slept in baby-innocence,—will have a charm that nothing else can rival. He may have tried to think the world his home, and live the life of the gay cosmopolitan; but when he has exhausted every other source of interest or affection, he will turn to the little room where his childish prattle first fell on a mother's ear, or he felt a father's proud caress.

"By the soft green light in the weedy glade,
   On the banks of moss where thy childhood play'd;
By the household tree through which thine eye
   First look'd in love to the summer sky;

By the dewy gleam, by the very breath
Of the primrose tufts in the grass beneath,
Upon thy heart there is laid a spell,
Holy and precious; oh, guard it well!

By the sleepy ripple of the stream,
Which hath lulled thee into many a dream,
By the shiver of the ivy-leaves
To the wind of morn at thy casement eaves,
By the bees' deep murmur in the limes,
By the music of the Sabbath chimes,
By every sound of thy native shade,
Stronger and dearer the spell is made.

By the gathering round the winter hearth,
When twilight call'd unto household mirth;
By the fairy tale or the legend old
In that ring of happy faces told;
By the quiet hour when hearts unite
In the parting prayer and the kind "good-night;
By the smiling eye and the loving tone,
O'er thy life has the spell been thrown.

And bless that gift, it hath gentle might,
A guardian power and a guiding light;
It hath led the freeman forth to stand
In the mountain battles of his land;
It hath brought the wanderer o'er the seas
To die on the hills of his own fresh breeze;
And back to the gates of his father's hall,
It hath led the weeping prodigal.

Yes, when thy heart in its pride may stray
From the pure first-loves of its youth away;

When the sullying breath of the world would come
O'er the flowers it brought from its childhood's home.
Think of thy sports at thy father's door,
And the kindly spell shall have power once more."

I had much to tell when I reached home,—
the daily mode of life at the Institution. the
studies we had, and our various other occupations—for all of which I found ready listeners.
They never seemed to weary hearing what I
had passed through while absent from them;
the process by which we learned to read; how
we were instructed in music; and, besides,
many employments useful and ornamental,
with which we were made familiar, such as the
making of fancy baskets with beads, knitting,
crocheting, and ever so many other handicrafts.
Then our amusements and our expedients for
physical exercise were recounted. All these
subjects were extremely interesting to them,
and many a long Summer day was beguiled of
its tediousness by their narration.

CHAPTER XVII.

"Unto this harvest ground
　　Proud reapers came,
Some for that strirring sound,
　　A warrior's name:

Some for the stormy play,
　　And joy of strife,
And some to fling away
　　A weary life."
　　　　　　　　Felicia Hemans.

"No more the drum
Provokes to arms, or trumpet's clangor shrill
Affrights the wives, or chills the maiden's blood;
But peace and plenty open to the view.
　　　　　　　　Philips.

"Talk not of comfort, 'tis for lighter ills;
I will indulge my sorrows, and give way
To all the pangs and fury of despair."
　　　　　　　　Addison's Cato.

Father was frequently in receipt of letters from my cousin, Louis F. Koester, who had for some years been residing in Charleston, South Carolina. He had become wealthy, and desired brother Fred should live with him. Cousin Louis was a wholesale grocer, and he thought it would be a good opening for Fred, if he would become a clerk in his store. It appeared an advantageous opportunity, and father acceded to the proposition. When vacation was over I returned to school, and Charles and Fred accompanied me to Baltimore. Fred left the day following for Charleston.

In a short time the war between the Southern and Northern States broke out. All communication by mail was cut off, and we were sadly distressed. Could we have foreseen this event, we should not have been willing for Fred to go South. We now feared we should not see him or hear from him for a long time. The suspense would be painful, and we deeply regretted the separation.

We waited long and anxiously for intelligence. Two years after the opening of the war, the Southern troops entered Maryland. We hoped to find Fred among them. We had learned that he had enlisted in the army early in the struggle. After the battles of Antietam and South Mountain, he came home. The meeting was a joyful one; we had dreaded lest we should hear of his death. But he had been spared, and was restored to his family once more. I was not at home to participate in the welcome and the thanksgiving upon his return; but he wrote to me, and his letter made me feel as if I were with them all. We had prayed that he might be spared, when the bullets rained thick around him, and the air was full of death. We had thought of him anxiously and tearfully when he could hear only the roar of the loud-mouthed cannon, the sharp clash of steel, or the mixed din and clangor of the battle-field. But he had been preserved; the God of battles had shielded him. He had several times been in the thickest of the fight. He had seen comrade after comrade fall at his side; had heard their death-moan, and caught the last faint message of love for the dear ones at home; then he had dashed again into the fight, leaving dying friends to their fate. Such is dreadful war.

Fred pictured many of the harrowing scenes, which he had witnessed. The recital drew tears from eyes that were not often suffused with emotion's tender moisture. He also described the fascination a battle had for the combatants. The listeners almost held their breath in terror, while he seemed to see only glory in the terrible encounter. These things were written to me, and very vivid letters they were. Mother and Fred both tried to give me

14

every detail as I could not be with them to hear for myself. I felt surprised that my brother had made so many hairbreadth escapes and yet had come through all uninjured,— surely he had been most mercifully preserved. I felt how good God was to take care of him and send him back to us.

For two summers during the war both armies made raids through Middletown Valley, laying waste its green fields, and scattering havoc everywhere. The people met with great losses; their various stores of grain for home consumption were exhausted. What a fearful thing is war, though it comes with colors flying and with the merry sound of drum and fife. Orphaned children and wailing widows, sad mothers and lonely sisters, mingle their lament with the shout of victory.

In September of 1862, the Southern Army made the first raid into the Valley. The inhabitants were greatly alarmed, as terrible disasters had everywhere followed, for the people upon whom the incursions were made. Many men fled from their families into other States for fear of being forced into the army. In a few days the village and the country around were filled with soldiers; the rattle of artillery and the general confusion that ensued changed the usual character of the quiet place and made it a very Bedlam. They demanded rations, which were given as far as the people had it in their power. The men offered to pay for what they received, but they had only Confederate money, which was of no value in the Valley. In less than a week the Union Army made its appearance. The Southerners proceeded westward to South Mountain, three and a half miles from Middletown. They had a skirmish a short distance from the village which compelled the people to take refuge in the cellars, while the shells were flying overhead. Some few soldiers were killed, but no serious results followed to the residents

Early next morning the battle of South Mountain commenced. Both armies fought vigorously all day. The noise and smoke of cannon were overpowering. The people were greatly terrified and the whole scene was appalling. The armies then proceeded to Antietam where the fight was renewed, lasting two days. The dead and dying were brought back to our village, now marred by war's devastating power. They were placed in the churches, school-houses, in private dwellings, and in the barns of the residents. Those who had "fought their last fight" were laid away in their nameless graves; while the living were tenderly cared for by the hospitable villagers.

The noble kindness of the people left a lasting impression upon those who lived to return to their homes in the different States, and in many instances their grateful remembrance was shown. In the summer of 1864 a second raid was made, again by the two armies in succession, and resulted in the almost utter impoverishment of the people. The farmers were stripped of their stock, their horses, their grain, indeed the place once so flourishing was left a barren waste. After, however, the armies had crossed the Potomac into Virginia, calm was restored, and every effort was made to repair the damage that had been done.

Many a soldier with tearful eye will speak of those, who, like the good Samaritan, poured oil into his wounds; lifted him when fallen by the wayside; then sent him with gentle wishes to his distant home.

War is a costly thing, not alone in a country's gold, flung wide by every boom from the cannon's throat; not alone in the embellishments that make up its tinselry and show; not alone in the lives that fall a sacrifice to the bloodthirsty god; but in the wrecked hopes of those who sit at home in loneliness, and whose wrung hearts have been wholly given up to sorrow and deep despair. This is the cost of war, too often the price paid for peace. We may here recall the sad plaint of one heart robbed of its treasures; nor will we overpaint the picture.

"A woman paced with hurried step, her lone and dreary cell;
The setting sun, with golden ray, upon her dark hair fell,
Which lay disheveled on her breast and many a shred of gray,
Wound midst those tresses—sorrow's gift, while on her breast they lay.

She murmured disconnected strains, as to and fro she paced,
And wildly beamed her piercing eye, and on her wasted face
A burning flush of fever glowed; then rolled the lava tide
Of thought from those thin pallid lips, as passionate she cried;
"Peace, peace, they tell me peace has come, they say the war is o'er;
The battle-cry the shriek of death shall fill the land no more·

They bid my heart rejoice, be glad, they bid my tears
    to cease;
Yes, yes my heart! thou shouldst rejoice, for thou hast
    paid for peace.

Ah! let me count the price once more, for fear my
    lips restrain
The faintest note that they should give to that rejoic-
    ing strain.
I had a son, a noble boy, just entered manhood's
    bloom,
But he forgot his mother's tears when first the cannon's
    boom
Was heard upon our nation's shores; ah! 'twas a
    magic spell,
And gallantly he bore our flag, and gallantly he fell.
I never saw my boy again, (they say my tears must
    cease,)
But, Herbert, drop for drop with thine, my heart paid
    blood for peace!"

"Another son, a stripling boy, who, always by my side,
Frail as a lily, was content forever to abide; not
    eighteen
Summers had I nursed with all a mother's care,
This tender plant, when orders came my only child
    to tear
From my embrace; I knew he'd die, and on my bended
    knee
I begged his life; besought and wept; but no, it could
    not be;
They bore him off. He never met the foe on hill or
    plain,
But drooped and died, I knew not where; we never
    met again.

O Willie, with thy soft blue eyes! Hush, hush, my
    heart must cease,
Yet darling with thy dying groans, I paid in part for
    peace!

"Now both were gone, who was left? None but the
    fond true heart
Who'd mingled tear for tear with mine—he who had
    borne a part
In every anguish wild which still my bosom rent,
Whose eyes were dim, whose hair was gray, with
    nights of weeping spent
For these our sons. I thought that we through all
    this midnight gloom,
Would, hand in hand, walk mournfully together to
    the tomb.

But war, insatiate, claimed him, too; I saw him, too,
    depart,
And something made of stone, I think, was given me
    for a heart;
I could not weep for many a day; I was alone,
With that cold weight within my breast—that heavy
    heart of stone.

Tears came and melted it at last; in prison far away,
Weary and worn, uncared for, too, he languished day
    by day;
But Herbert and our Willie came, and bade the cap-
    tive go;
They broke his chains, I know they did, the angels
    told me so;
And when they bore his soul aloft, and bade his suf-
    ferings cease,
I paid in spirit on his grave all that I owed for peace."

"Must I rejoice? perchance I might; but was that all
    the price?
Ah! did my jewels, did my tears, my broken heart
    suffice?
No! count upon the battle-field ten thousand name-
    less graves;
Call on the winds for sighs and groans; go tell the
    ocean waves
To bring their dead; the prison walls to shriek their
    sickening tales.
Concentrate, if you've power to-night, widow's and
    orphan's wails;
Heap broken hearts on broken hearts, till pity bid
    you cease,
And then you'll have not half the price that we have
    paid for peace."

This, it is true, is a sketch not based upon
fact; but its counterpart was to be found in
many a home when the roll of heavy artillery
had died off to a whisper, then was silent, for
the contest was ended, and peace was won.
There are bleeding hearts to-day, and purpose-
less intellects, whose unwritten history if told,
would be as thrilling as any tale of woe, imagination's wildest frenzy ever penned.

CHAPTER XVIII.

"True happiness
Consists not in the multitude of friends,
But in the worth and choice."
                    Jonson's Cynthia's Revels.

"There are moments of life that we never forget,
  Which brighten and brighten, as time steals away;
They give a new charm to the happiest lot,
  And they shine on the gloom of the loneliest day."
                    J. G. Percival.

"Long, long be my heart with such memories fill'd!
  Like the vase in which roses have once been distill'd,
You may break, you may ruin the vase, if you will,
  But the scent of the roses will hang round it still."
                    Moore.

"Life's a short summer—man a flower,
  He dies—alas! how soon he dies!"
                    Dr. Johnson.

The South had suffered greatly by the war,
and business prospects were so unpromising
that brother Fred determined not to return,
but to try and find employment elsewhere.
He decided to make an effort to settle in Baltimore. He had learned watchmaking, and
concluded now he would make practical use of
his knowledge. With this object in view, he

15

wrote to Charles and myself, and we felt glad to have another of our family near us. It made the place still more homelike.

About this time, Mr. Keener resigned the position of Superintendent, the office being too confining. He had done much towards advancing the general prosperity of the Institution. Among the many improvements he had suggested and carried into successful operation, was the securing of maps adapted to the use of the blind. The pupils felt indebted to him for the kind personal interest he had in them. He had always been friendly and considerate, and was in every respect a christian gentleman. In retiring from the Superintendency, he took with him the warm regards of all, and their kindest wishes for success in whatever path in life he might choose. Sincere prayers from grateful hearts were offered, that his future might be smiled upon by Providence, as his past had been, in the fruition of good works.

About five years after he had sundered his relationship to us, Mr. Keener accepted the office of Superintendent of the Navassa Guano Island, in the West Indies. And on his return to Baltimore after a long absence, he called to see me; he had not forgotten me, though he had passed through such varied scenes since I was under his care; I appreciated the visit highly.

It is with deep regret that I note the recent death of this gentleman. On the 9th of November, 1872, far from his native land, among strangers he passed away from earth.

Many tears fell when the sad intelligence came—not only from sightless eyes:—He was known and loved at the Boys' Home, the Manual Labor School, and at the House of Refuge. He died at the age of forty-three years; little more than mid way up life's rugged steep—but if the works of a life mark its period, he had attained a green old age.

Upon Mr. Keener's resignation, Mr. F. D. Morrison was given charge of the Institution. He entered upon his duties with evident earnestness; and showed immediately deep interest in our welfare. He addressed himself with great persistency of purpose to the securing of more complete accommodations as well as generally more commodious arrangements for the pupils. A new building had been talked of for some time, but its accomplishment seemed a thing of the indefinite future. Our new Superintendent felt not so, and set to work to attain the desired object at an early day. He took active measures to secure the result, and in his appeals for aid was untiring. In a few years our new home was completed. This beautiful edifice is located on Boundary avenue, and is the one of which previous mention has been made, a monument of benevolence in the City of Monuments.

During my stay in the Institution, I attended the Third Reformed Church, of which Rev. J. S. Foulk was pastor. I connected myself with the Sunday school. Mrs. L. Byrne was my teacher; this lady was devoted to her class, and we reaped great benefit from her instruction and advice. Her single purpose was to do good. We all became much attached to her. She tried to impress on our youthful minds the duty we owed Him from whom we received our every blessing. She plead with us to observe how great His loving kindness and tender mercy, though He chastened. I shall never forget how she strove to show us the influence our example would have upon others; and how she urged us so to live that we might be patterns of excellence in every respect. Had we been faithful to her pious teachings, we should have made fewer crooked paths in our life-journeying. Her memory will ever be cherished gratefully and fondly. Her precepts and holy example were instruments in inducing many a little one to strive to be a faithful Christian.

Dr. Foulk and his family were always kind and attentive to me. They visited me frequently, and gave many practical evidences of their solicitude. Remembrances of these friends are among the most precious of my life.

While a pupil in the Institution, I was confirmed, and have continued my membership of the Church, so tenderly associated with the first years of my affliction. Dr. Foulk has since accepted a call to Carlisle, Pennsylvania, and is there esteemed and beloved by his people as he was in Baltimore. I doubt not he will have many stars in his crown of rejoicing, when, earth's labors ended, he shall put on immortality's robes.

Quite a number of pupils from the Institution joined the school, making two large classes. Mrs. Byrne had charge of the girls, and Mr. Alfred George of the boys. Both these teachers were unremitting in their efforts to be of service to their scholars; and God crowned each Sabbath day with some mark of His approval. Mrs. Byrne and Mr.

George regarded it a privilege to be eyes for
the blind in their search for the truths of Holy
Writ; and with glad hearts they beheld religion's calm and peaceful light illumine the
faces of those whose outer vision obscured,
could yet look upon the glory of Him who
reigneth on high, revealed in saving grace.

Mr. George, in the midst of his usefulness,
was snatched away by death. At his grave
there were no sincerer mourners than those
who, when in heaven they met, should, for the
first time see the friend who, as an honored instrument in God's hand, had shed religion's
pure light on their way. Their voices were
tremulous with emotion as they joined in the
exultant strain,—

> "I would not live alway,
> No! welcome the tomb;
> Since Jesus hath lain there,
> I dread not its gloom.
> There sweet be my rest,
> Till He bid me arise
> To hail Him in triumph,
> Ascending the skies."

Many other of our church relationships were
of a kind affectionate character. Members of
the choir aided us in learning anniversary

hymns. On one of these occasions seventeen of our pupils were presented each with a copy of the Bible, in raised letters. This was a priceless treasure to the recipient, dearer the more closely we studied the sacred pages. Years of possession could only add to its value, for as the cares of the world crowded into our lives, where could be found surer comfort than in the sympathy of one " who was a man of sorrows and acquainted with grief?" Our gratitude was tearfully expressed, for we could but weep, though our hearts were full of gladness too.

The presentation was made by Francis T. King, President of the Maryland Bible Society, *the friend* who is a friend indeed. His heart is ever ready to respond to humanity's call. This gentleman is ubiquitous in his connection with every good work. He is indeed remarkable for his ready sympathy, and practical aid in all the charities of our city. God's blessing must surely follow him.

The gift would ever be a treasured reminder of our church associations as well as of the generous donors who found it in their hearts to bestow it.

I frequently received letters from my friend,

Mr. Cole. He counselled me to be diligent and persevering, warning me against losing one opportunity of acquiring knowledge. I strove to act upon his advice, and found it greatly to my advantage to do so. Mr. Cole married, and during his wedding tour visited Baltimore. He and his wife called upon me, at the Institution; I read and played for them, and they appeared much pleased with my progress. They cordially invited me to spend my next vacation, in Shippensburg, Pa., where they were to reside. Mrs. Cole was very affectionate in manner, this won my heart at once, particularly as her husband had been such a good friend to me. She had a sweet voice, which made me think her gentle and winning; and her pleasant good-bye fell like music on my ear.

With the blind, there is much in the tone of voice to attract or repel. They are so sensitive in this particular, that they often judge character from this special endowment; and, although it may seem strange, and to some even incredible, they are oftener accurately impressed than the contrary. It is natural, if not always safe to conclude that a voice is influenced by the impulses of the heart. A sweet voice is always a grace. A low voice is eloquent in love, in sorrow, or in despair. A harsh sinister voice, and one like the clicking of a steel trap are unmistakeable in their indications. We all have heard tones, whose depth and richness were the signs of power, either of intellect or passion. "A still small voice" uttered "peace be still," and the angry waves of Galilee were calm. So ofttimes have the subdued tones of affection quelled the rising storm of passion in the human breast, and bade it "peace be still." But we will not longer dwell upon the varied power of the human voice. It was God's great gift to man, when he breathed the breath of life into his nostrils, and man became a living soul, endowed with reason, supreme above the brute creation to whom instinct without speech was assigned.

Various changes had taken place in the Institution. Prof. H. H. Bruning, one of our teachers, a gentleman of excellent scholastic attainments had resigned, intending to open an Academy of his own in Lancaster, Pa. He had been succeeded by Miss Mary Patrick, who was our teacher but a few months, when she was married. We rejoiced in her happiness, as she had endeared herself to us during the

short time we had been her pupils.   Mrs. Jane
Arnold had been connected with the Institution about five years, when death removed her
from us.   She had been both friend and teacher
and her loss was deeply mourned.   Thus it is,
" friend after friend departs," and we miss them
from our midst.   There must always be one
chord to sorrow strung, else the harmony would
be incomplete.   The sad minor key is the
undertone of all our spirits' lives, and it has a
plaintive charm for every one, even if heard in
youth's gay morning hour.

Prof. Wm. Harman had been our teacher
of music for some time, and was beloved by all
the pupils.   He was a thorough instructor, and
those who fulfilled his requirements could not
fail to attain proficiency.   Upon his resignation, Prof. Barrington was appointed by the
Board of Trustees.   This gentleman enjoyed
an excellent reputation, which he has since
admirably sustained.   The progress of his
pupils has been of the most satisfactory character; and he is withal very genial in manner,
calculated to win the friendly regard of those
whom he instructs, as well as their willing
application to duty.

The positions held by Mrs. Arnold and Miss

Patrick when left vacant, were filled by Miss
Emma and Miss Louise Yarnall   These ladies
were eminently fitted for the responsibilities
they assumed.   Lovely in character and well
qualified as teachers, they could only be desir-
able acquisitions to the Institution   We cherished fondly the memory of those who had
providentially been removed from us, yet, wo
could but feel happy in our new relations.

CHAPTER XIX.

"Human life is chequer'd at the best,
And joy and grief alternately preside."
Tracy.

"Friendship! mysterious cement of the soul!
Sweet'ner of life, and solder of society!
I owe thee much. Thou has deserved of me
Far, far beyond what I can ever pay.
Oft have I prov'd the labors of thy love;
And the warm effort of the gentle heart,
Anxious to please."
Blair.

"The friends thou hast and their adoption tried,
Grapple them to thy soul with hooks of steel."
Shakspere's Hamlet.

"There is no fount
Of deep, strong, deathless love, like that within
A mother's heart."
Mrs. Heman's Siege of Valencia.

While many changes were taking place in
the Institution, in my family also events had
occurred in which I was deeply interested.
Charles had removed to Charleston and had
gone into the grocery business. Fred had
married and was living in Richmond. My
sister Maria had married and settled in Balti-

more. Portions of our family were now living in South Carolina, Virginia and Maryland, not very widely scattered it is true, yet we were far enough apart to make it scarcely probable we should be again an undivided household. We should henceforth miss some who had shared with us the joys of home. Father and mother realized this, but they believed all to have been directed by a kind Providence, for blessings had followed their children, more than they had asked. To each it is true " some days had been dark and dreary," still there had been many, many bright days for which to be thankful.

Brother Charles' health began to fail, and it was thought the climate possibly did not suit him, so he concluded to try what effect a trip North would have. He wrote asking Fred to take charge of his business for him. This arrangement having been satisfactorily made, he started on the proposed trip. He visited a number of places and received great benefit. He remained longest at Cape May, and found the sea bathing very invigorating. He returned home much improved in health, and fearing to lose the good he had gained, decided not to go to Charleston again, but to wind up his

business there and locate in Middletown. At
this time he purchased me a piano, which
generous gift was most acceptable, for I had
become devotedly fond of music and spent
many solitary hours, losing my sense of loneliness in the companionship of sweet sounds.

My father had been fortunate in business, and
was now able to purchase property in Middletown. God had prospered him, and he enjoyed
the pleasant prospect of being able in his old
age to sit down under his "own vine and fig-
tree." It is sad when misfortune and vicissitude
fall on any lot, but saddest of all when they
come with declining years, as the foot begins
to step tremblingly, or the hand be unsteady
in its palsied grasp, the head whitened with
the frosts of many winters, and the form bowed
with the burdens it has borne. It is meet that
those, who have been spared such a close to the
toil of a lifetime, should be very thankful.
Father felt this, and night and morning, at the
family altar, he acknowledged God's bountiful
goodness to him, in having acknowledged the
labor of his hands so abundantly.

My time at school was rapidly drawing to a
close. I had been in the Institution nearly
eight years, all of which had been very happy

years, and so swiftly had they flown I could hardly believe them more than months. I had made many dear friends, to be cherished while life should last. Nor were these tender ties formed only with the teachers and pupils, but with persons outside. Among the latter are some I shall ever remember. Mr. William Ball's family were kind and thoughtful at all times. I spent many happy hours with them. One sad association drew me near them, Little Ida, a pet with all who knew her, and her grandpa's darling, a fair-haired child, sprightly and interesting in manner, was blind. She was born sightless, and this fact appealed strongly to my sympathy. To her parents it had made her doubly dear.

Mrs. Maynard and family also were good friends of mine. Indeed these two families were continually studying how they could contribute to my comfort and enjoyment. Nor did they forget my schoolmates, but in many thoughtful acts and attentions added to their pleasures. Very many others than myself, in all the future, will look back gratefully upon their kindly offices. These allusions are very personal, I am well aware, but they are "green spots," and are refreshing to think upon.

You, gentle reader, will pardon, for you are not following a life, in which there need be the observance of any special conventional form, but that of a blind girl; whose heart having known sorrow and bereavement, still, as the drooping flower drinks in the dew and sunlight, then rejoices, accepts the bright things of her lot in deep thankfulness.

I was soon to leave my home in the Institution and the friends I had made, while there. Although I knew my parents were longing for my return, I felt reluctant to go. A new world had been opened to my inward vision, during my stay in Baltimore. My plans and purposes had materially changed. I now looked forward to usefulness in the world, not in any wide sense of the term, but according to my ability. I experienced a stimulus in living I had not known before, and which bereft of sight as I was I should never have been aware of, had it not been for the opportunities of mental improvement I had enjoyed.

My parents anticipated my return very gladly. They longed that I should again be with them. Except the vacation seasons I had been absent from them eight years. My mother's health was much impaired, she was confined to her

room a great part of the time. I hoped to be
of some service to her, if only to make the
hours pass less wearily by telling her what I
had learned in many ways since last with her.
To an invalid even the minutes drag a slow
length along and hours and days seem ages if
pain rack the feeble body. I thought by my
music to interest my mother and call her attention sometimes from her sufferings.

It is a holy office to be able to give back to
a mother part of the love and care she bestowed upon us in helpless infancy. It is a
pious trust and one that, well fulfilled, will
bring sweet content in years to come, when the
loved one may be sleeping sweetly beneath the
swaying cypress or the lilies fair. Mother-
love taken from us can never be replaced, once
lost, it is forever gone, save as it blooms again
in Paradise. Earth is lonelier, home is void
when her feet have stepped into the river of
death. Our hearts have no nestling place "like
the bosom first pressed," if her heart has ceased
to beat; and we pause on life's highway, missing the guardian angel of our young years,.to
plead, as the stilly twilight comes softly on,

"Backward, turn backward, oh Time, in your flight,
  Make me a child again just for to-night;
    16

Over my heart in the days that are flown,
No love like mother-love ever has shone,—
No other worship abides and endures,
Faithful, unselfish and patient like yours,—
None like a mother can charm away pain
From the sick soul and world-weary brain."

Well may we cherish the precious treasure, the sweetest boon God ever gave; with gentle care enfold the wasting form, with loving hand guide the feeble steps, and in every way strive to make the sunset of a mother's life full of beauty, blending tints of softer light with those of richer loveliness. Her last days, even if passed in bodily anguish, may be the fullness of joy if crowned and blessed with the love of her children.

Worse than the brute must that man or woman be who can forget the sacred duty, of filial care and tenderness for a mother. If any eye should rest on these pages, which if turned inward, finds one thought of disrespect for a mother's counsel, thrust it out, for it is a dark spot, that when the pall shall have been settled on the dead mother, no tears of regret will ever wash out.

The hour of parting from my school friends came; I can never forget it. My heart was deeply stirred for I was sundering relationships

not again to be entered into. I was leaving a
life behind that had been full of genial incident to take up another that must have sterner
experiences in it, than any period of the past,
as I should try the world; and its lessons are
ever hard to learn. New duties and responsibilities awaited me. The occasion was to me
one of unusual significance.

My associates expressed sorrow that we were
to be separated, and the trembling voice indi-
cated the sincerity of their words of parting.
We who had walked so long together, the light
of our faces hid from each other, were now to
take a divided way. We had looked for this,
but always in the future; now it had come,
and with it brought its trial. Brother Charles
was to take me home; when he came, I bade
a last and tearful adieu to the Institution, my
teachers, schoolmates, and friends. The years
passed there were henceforth to be a memory
with a radiant halo round it—" a joy forever."

CHAPTER XX.

"The dear beatitudes of home,
  Within the heavenly boundaries come:
  The hearts that made life's fragrance here,
  To Eden haunts bring added cheer;
  And all the beauty, all the good,
  Lost to our lower altitude,
  Transfigured, yet the same, are given
  Upon the mountain-heights of heaven."

Lucy Larcom.

"Do not forever with thy veiléd lids,
  Seek for thy noble father in the dust;
  Thou know'st 'tis common; all that live must die,
  Passing through nature to eternity."

Shakspere.

"The hearth, the hearth, is desolate,—the fire is quenched
    and gone,
  That into happy children's eyes once brightly laughing
    shone,
  The place where mirth and music met is hush'd through
    day and night,
  O! for one kind, one sunny face, of all that here made
    light !
      *   *   *   *   *   *
  The father's voice—the mother's prayer—though called
    from earth away—
  With music ringing from the dead, their spirits yet shall
    sway;

And by the past, and by the grave, the parted yet are
  one,
Though the loved hearth be desolate, the bright fire
  quench'd and gone."

                      Felicia Hemans.

  My parents were rejoiced to have me at home
again. My mother wept for joy, I wept also,
but mine were tears of mingled joy and sorrow. For weeks after my return, I thought of
scarcely anything else than the Institution and
its many pleasant associations. My father sympathized with me; when he attended the military school in Germany, he became much
attached to it, and upon leaving felt great regret. My parents promised me I should visit
Baltimore, a few weeks before school closed
for the summer vacation, so that I might meet
my friends again before they left for their various homes. This delighted me and I felt
more reconciled to the change in my surroundings and mode of living.

  Mother was very ill during the following
winter. Sometimes we thought she could
hardly rally, she was so prostrated. She had
no fear of death, but appeared to look forward to it as a happy release from suffering.
Her perfect resignation was a great comfort to
us and tended to allay the apprehension we

constantly experienced. When Spring came again, her health improved and she could once more go out of doors and enjoy the invigorating sunlight. This was a great happiness to us, and we grew hopeful of a still further recovery.

Brother Charles decided to make another change, this time he concluded to go West. He intended to start in the tobacco business. Thus a welcome to a returning member of our family was followed by a fond good bye to one departing. We regretted to have our brother leave us but it seemed for the best, so we strove to utter no word of discouragement, but to bid him " God speed " in his undertaking.

According to the promise made me I was soon to go to Baltimore, the Summer was rapidly approaching, and when it had surely come I was to be again for a short time with my school friends. I could not wait patiently. I started two weeks before the close of the scholastic year. I had a most delightful visit, all my expectations were realized and I had looked forward to a great deal of pleasure. I remained in the city, a few weeks with my married sister. While there I received a letter from father stating mother was very ill and

that he feared she would not recover. This
was painful as well as startling news, for we
had thought she was getting better.

To add to my distress I could not at once
get to my mother. The memorable flood, which
occurred at this time, had destroyed the rail-
roads. I was compelled to remain in Baltimore, enduring the most terrible suspense.

While anxiously waiting for the means of
travel again to be available, I was shocked by
the receipt of a despatch, announcing my father's death. This was a most unlooked for
event and overwhelmed me with its sudden-
ness. We could not believe the sad intelligence. We thought there must have been a
mistake in forwarding the telegram and that
our mother was meant. In his letter received
but a short time before, father had said all the
family were well, but mother. We felt sure
an error had been made in wording the message.

The bridges had been repaired the day before
we received the despatch; so we started for
home on the first train, in this uncertain state
of mind, and weighed down with sorrow at
our affliction in either event. On arriving in
Frederick, sister hired a conveyance to take us

to Middletown.   As we entered the house I
thought I heard my father's voice saying "the
girls have come."   But alas! he was cold in
death.   He had no welcome for us, his lips
were sealed in the hush of everlasting silence.

Our mother was lying at the point of death.
We found a number of friends endeavoring to
comfort her in her heavy bereavement.   Father
had been stricken suddenly; when attacked he
was apparently in his usual good health.   The
severe pain he endured, cramped his body vio-
lently for thirty hours.   Besides his physical
sufferings his mental distress was most poig-
nant.   My uncle was with him and grasping
his hand, father said—" Oh, dear brother, I am
going to die, how can I leave my afflicted
family!"   The physician strove faithfully but
without success to relieve his agony.   When
Rev. F. A. Rupley, his pastor, prayed that
strength might be given, and submission to the
will of God might be granted, father seemed
resigned.   Three hours before his death, he
fell into a deep sleep from which he never
awakened.   Mr. Rupley had continued pray-
ing with him till he breathed his last.

Father had been for many years a christian,
full of faith and good works.   He had taken

great pains to teach his children the truths of
the Bible, and had by an upright example en-
forced the precepts he had laid before them.
In disposition he had always been kind and
gentle. He was no more to be with us, the
light of his smile had gone out. Our hearts
were appalled with the magnitude of our loss.
So suddenly had the blow fallen that we could
not realize we were fatherless. It was as
if a painful dream had marred our pleasant
slumber. A few hours only had passed and
the hand that had penned warm loving words
was stiffened in death. What a lesson of life's
uncertainty, how brittle the thread by which it
is held! Our mother of whom he had written
had outlived him, she so long an invalid, and
he strong and well, hurried to the grave. The
dispensation was most mysterious, one we could
not hope to comprehend, till in Heaven we
know God's purposes; there all that we have
not understood shall be made plain.

We sorrowed not as those without hope, for
we knew in yon celestial country we should
meet our earthly parent again, a ransomed
spirit. He had been called from care and
strife and pain to rest with those "who had

17

come up through much tribulation, their robes washed white in the blood of the Lamb."

We tried to compose our feelings before entering mother's room, lest our grief might add to her distress. We found her greatly excited. She had talked more during father's brief illness than she had during month's previous, and as a consequence, was much exhausted. Father's sudden death had severely shocked her nervous system. She had not shed a tear but her deep sorrow was evident. She strove to bear with christian fortitude the trial. When we entered the room, she said—"children your father was dear to you and me, but God has seen fit to take him to Himself. We are sorely stricken, but God will comfort and sustain us, we must trust Him fully."

The funeral was to take place the following morning. Many friends came to take a last look at the face of the departed. Those who stood by the remains of our father drew a lesson from the silent form; it taught them, oh how forcibly, that "in the midst of life we are in death;" and they turned away with the solemn thought borne in upon their souls—"behold in such an hour as ye think not, the Son of Man cometh."

Mother had not seemed able to comprehend the whole extent of her loss; at first it stunned her, being in a very weak condition. She became worse than she had been, and every one felt her end was drawing near. She was too feeble to be taken in to see father; even the sad pleasure of a last kiss was denied her. When the funeral was about to leave the house, she desired to be moved near the window. She looked out with tearful eyes, and then a bright smile played upon her features as she murmured in low sweet tones the happy thought—"farewell my husband, but a little while and I shall join you in your heavenly land; we shall not long be severed, this is my great consolation."

The remains of our father were conveyed to the church, where the Rev. Mr. R. preached a very impressive sermon from Mark, 13th chap., 37th verse—"What I say unto you, I say unto all, Watch." After the ceremonies were ended at the church, with sad hearts, and yet not mourning as those without hope, we followed our beloved parent to his last resting place. Having reached the cemetery we laid him in the grave, then slowly returned to our desolate home.

A few days after my father's burial we saw

that mother was rapidly failing. She asked us not to mourn for her, she was willing to die, for she would then be united again to her husband. She said rather than grieve that she was going to leave us, we should pray for her speedy release from pain that she might find rest in Heaven. Her sufferings were great, and there seemed to be no alleviation for them, yet in the selfishness of our love, we could not bear to give her up. Now that we had lost father, she was doubly dear to us.

After an interval of extreme pain, she fell asleep, and so continued for fourteen hours. Every effort was made to arouse her, for we feared it would prove her long last sleep. When we succeeded in awaking her, she appeared composed, though fully aware that she was passing from us. She recognized all around her, smiled lovingly upon us, and in almost inarticulate words bade us meet her in Heaven. Then she breathed her life away so calmly and sweetly—the departing spirit faded off so slowly that only by the changed expression of the face, the loss of pain and the quickly following heavenly gleam, could we tell that she had gone from earth to join the loved and lost, in a better land. Her prayer was answered that she might not long be separated from our father. We laid her beside him, then left the quiet mounds; bereft of both our parents, the once dear home was now a vacant shrine.

In my sightless loneliness I should find all joys less, now that my mother could no longer cheer me. From my life had been taken its strong stay, and ever as the years rolled on I should mourn :—

"The May sun sheds an amber light
  On new leaved woods and lawns between;
But she who, with a smile more bright,
  Welcomed and watched the springing green,
      Is in her grave,
      Low in her grave.

The fair white blossoms of the wood
  In groups beside the pathway stand;
But one, the gentle and the good,
  Who cropped them with a fairer hand,
      Is in her grave,
      Low in her grave.

Upon the woodland's morning airs
  The small birds mingled notes are flung;
But she whose voice more sweet than theirs,
  Once bade me listen while they sung,
      Is in her grave,
      Low in her grave.

That music of the early year
  Brings tears of anguish to my eyes;
My heart aches when the flowers appear,
  For then I think of her who lies
    Within her grave,
    Low in her grave."

The loss of a mother is one every heart is likely to experience; yet this does not make the trial less. We may see her fade daily, but we turn from the painful truth, and watching anxiously, hail with a thrill of joy, hope's faintest message.

"Oh many lips are saying
  Mid falling tears to-day;
And many hearts are aching sore,
  Our mother's passed away;
We watched her fading year by year,
  As they went slowly by,
But cast far from us e'en the fear
  That she could ever die.

She seemed so good, so pure, so true
  To our admiring eyes,
We never dreamed this glorious fruit
  Was ripening for the skies;
And when at last the death stroke came,
  So swift, so sure, so true,
The hearts that held her here so fast,
  Were almost broken too.

We robed her in familiar dress,
  We smoothed her soft hair down,

Gave one last kiss, then laid her 'mid
  The autumn leaves so brown;
Then each took up the broken thread
  Of life and all its cares,
How sad the thought 'mid daily tasks,
  We miss our mother's prayers.

We ne'er shall know from what dark paths
  They may have kept our feet;
Yet holy will their influence be
  While each fond heart shall beat:
And as we tread the thorny way,
  Which her dear feet have trod,
Ever shall feel our mother's prayers
  Leading us up to God."

CHAPTER XXI.

"Oh! what a change comes over that sad heart,
    Where all was joyous, light, and free from care,
All thoughts of peace do for a time depart,
    And yield to grief, and anguish, and despair."
                                    J. T. Watson.

"His sweetest dreams were still
Of that dear voice that soothed his infancy."
                                    Robert Southey.

"Voice after voice hath died away,
    Once in my dwelling heard,
Sweet household name by name hath chang'd
    To grief's forbidden word!
From dreams of night on each I call,
    Each of the far remov'd;
And waken to my own wild cry,
    Where are ye, my belov'd?"
                                    Felicia Hemans.

After our mother's funeral, and the kind
friends who had ministered to us in our sorrow, had left us, sister Maria returned to her
home in Baltimore. Brother Andrew, sister
Minnie and I remained. We were lonely and
disconsolate. As we pondered upon the trials
we had passed through our hearts sank within
us. But we took comfort in the remembrance

of our parents' lives and their calm and holy deaths. We recalled teachings which to us had "priceless been." Though now Providence seemed estranged, yet we trusted that all was for our good. Strength was given by which we were enabled to bear our double loss with meek submission.

We had written to Charles and Fred the sad news of our parents' death. In a few days we received a letter from Fred stating that he and his family had been ill for some weeks. All were greatly shocked at the unexpected intelligence we had sent them, they could with difficulty believe it. Even the youngest child felt the blow. Brother Andrew decided to go to Hagerstown and engage in business; sister Minnie and myself were left the only occupants of a home, a short time before so full of cheerfulness, but where now sadness reigned supreme.

A number of weeks had passed without our hearing from Charles. We were sure he had not heard of the events so recently occurring or he would have written. When some nine weeks had elapsed we received a letter from him directed to father. It read thus—Dear Parents: It has been some months since I

heard from you. Since then I have travelled
through the greater part of the Western States.
I am now in Detroit, Michigan. The cause
of my delay in writing to you, has been the
uncertainty of my business arrangements. I
have found no suitable opening.

Your loving son—CHARLES.

After Charles left home we had frequently
received discouraging letters from him. He
had been absent some months, and father had
written repeatedly, urging him to settle himself to some business and not wander from
place to place. He loved new scenes, and had
often said if he had means he would travel
over the world. A few days before father's
death, he wrote to Charles, strongly advising
him at once to strive to have definite objects in
view. He told him, he hoped when next he
heard from him, the advice he had so often
given, would have been acted upon. When
Charles' answer came, father and mother had
been some months buried.

Minnie and I were in doubt how to break
the news to him. We first thought of asking
him to come home, without telling him what
changes had taken place. Upon reflection we

abandoned this idea, as we feared he might postpone his return, if an opportunity of further travel occurred, and we might again lose all knowledge of his whereabouts. We consulted with friends as to what course we had best take, they advised our giving him the full particulars of all that had happened since he last heard from us, and to urge him to come and settle in Middletown in the old homestead.

One week later he was with us; he had started immediately after the receipt of our letter, remaining in Baltimore long enough to see sister Maria and learn from her any details we had omitted. He was overcome with grief. He would wander through the house from room to room, saying—"our home is indeed desolate." He remained with us but a few days. He could not endure seeing the many things that reminded him of our deceased parents. We thought it best he should find employment elsewhere in order that his mind might be occupied. He left us promising not to go further than Baltimore or Washington. In a few days we received a letter from him written from Washington; a week later we were surprised to hear from him in Detroit. This greatly perplexed us, but we could only submit.

Sister Maria wrote to us to dispose of the property to the best advantage we could and come and live with her. She was in delicate health and needed our services. The following Spring we left Middletown and went to Balti-more. We had heard from Charles some months back. He gave as his reason for having returned to Detroit without consulting us, that he hoped there to find relief for his sorrow which he had failed to do when near his former home; he believed we would try to dissuade him from going, so went without our knowledge. We wrote offering all the consolation we could and still requesting him to come back and locate near us.

We received no answer; we waited what we considered a sufficiently long time then we wrote to the gentleman with whom he was engaged in business. From him we learned Charles was very melancholy; often appeared sad and strange. He had done all he could to cheer him but without success. We wrote again urging him to come to us. A few weeks later we received a letter together with a Detroit paper, announcing our brother's death. Dear reader this added sorrow seemed more than I could bear. Charles had not always been a devoted son, but he had been to me a good and faithful brother, always loving, tender and generous. His heart was deeply touched by my affliction, and he strove in every way to add to my comfort and happiness. I was his favorite sister and he lavished gifts upon me. These I value beyond expression and hold as precious tokens of my brother's love.

The sudden death of our parents had shocked his nervous system so severely that his health was greatly impaired and his mind yielded to the pressure. He had always been of an extremely sensitive temperament, and never quite so strong physically as the rest of us. Eight months after our father's and mother's death, he sank into the grave, far from home, with strangers only near.

My heart was deeply riven. I felt all ties were sundering, earth seemed losing its every charm, but Heaven was growing dearer as I thought that there again I could be folded to a mother's heart, all sorrow past, all mourning over, all tears dried. My very soul thrilled with the longing for that new life which should restore what was lost and broken here. This

is a common sympathy, a universal aspiration ;
—for we feel the truth borne in upon us,—

   "Down below, the wild November whistling
      Through the beech's dome of burning red,
   And the Autumn sprinkling penitential
      Dust and ashes on the chestnut's head.

   Down below, a pall of airy purple,
      Darkly hanging from the mountain side,
   And the sunset from his eyebrows staring
      O'er the long roll of the leaden tide.

   Up above, the tree with leaf unfading,
      By the everlasting river's brink,
   And the sea of glass beyond whose margin
      Never yet the sun was known to sink.

   Down below, the white wings of the sea-bird
      Dashed across the furrows dark with mould,
   Flitting like the memories of our childhood,
      Through the trees now waxen pale and old.

   Down below imaginations quivering
      Through our human spirits like the wind,
   Thoughts that toss like leaves upon the woodland,
      Hopes like sea-birds flashed across the mind.

   Up above, the host no man can number,
      In white robes, a palm in every hand,
   Each some work sublime forever working,
      In the spacious tracts of that great land.

   Up above, the thoughts that know no anguish,
      Tender care, sweet love for us below,
   Noble pity free from anxious terror,
      Larger love without a touch of woe.

Down below, a sad mysterious music,
  Wailing through the woods and on the shore,
Burdened with a grand majestic secret,
  That keeps sweeping from us evermore.

Up above, a music that entwineth,
  With eternal threads of golden sound,
The great poem of this strange existence,
  All whose wondrous meaning hath been found.

Down below, the Church, to whose poor window,
  Glory by the autumnal trees is lent,
And a knot of worshippers in mourning,
  Missing some one at the Sacrament.

Up above, the burst of hallelujah,
  And (without the sacramental mist
Wrapt around us like a sunlit halo)
  One great vision of the face of Christ.

Down below, cold sunlight on the tombstone,
  And the green wet turf with faded flowers,
Winter roses, once like young hopes burning,
  Now beneath the ivy dripped with showers:

And the new made grave within the Churchyard,
  And the white cap on that dear face pale,
And the watcher ever as it dusketh
  Rocking to and fro with that long wail.

Up above, a crowned and happy spirit,
  Like an infant in the eternal years,
Who shall grow in love and light forever,
  Ordered in his place among his peers.

O, the sobbing of the winds of autumn,
  O, the desolate heart that grave above,
O, the white cap shaking as it darkens,
  Round that shrine of memory and love.

O, the rest forever, and the rapture!
  O, the hand that wipes the tears away!
O, the golden homes beyond the sunset,
  And the hope that watches o'er the clay!"

How eloquent the teaching, all humanity responds to it with loud voice and deep accord. We look from earth to heaven, and our hearts are lifted up from sorrow and filled with blissful contemplations of the glorious life awaiting us beyond the tomb.

CHAPTER XXII.

——"Death should come
Gently to one of gentle mould, like thee,
As light winds wandering through groves of bloom,
    Detach the delicate blossoms from the tree,
Close thy sweet eyes calmly, and without pain,
    And we will trust in God to see thee yet again."
                                    Bryant.

" Like the sweet melody which faintly lingers
    Upon the wind-harp's strings at close of day,
When gently touched by evening's dewy fingers
    It breathes a low and melancholy lay,
So the calm voice of sympathy me seemeth;
    And while its magic spell is round me cast,
My spirit in its cloister'd silence dreameth,
    And vaguely blends the future with the past."
                                    Mrs. Embury.

"So, at the loom of life, we weave
    Our separate shreds that varying fall,
Some stained, some fair; and passing leave
    To God, the gathering up of all."
                                    Lucy Larcom.

We had now another painful duty to perform, that of announcing to brother Fred, still
living in Charleston, the death of our brother.
We had seemed latterly only to have sad
tidings for him, and we dreaded writing.
18

Fred was of course much shocked, but bore the intelligence more resignedly than we had expected. We had known so many trials, that sorrow was losing its keenest edge, and we were able to bear more than we had supposed it possible we could. Our Heavenly Father had chastened us sorely, but He had been with us and we were not utterly cast down. We knew He would give us days of joy again though now sorrow was weighing heavily upon us.

Brother Fred determined to remove to Baltimore with his family. He found the southern climate very enervating, and as our number was now so lessened, he felt he would like the few remaining to be near each other. Sister Maria's health was failing fast; she had for some time shown symptoms of consumption, and her disease was progressing rapidly. We watched her day by day as the hectic flush heightened in her cheek and her hard dry cough increased. We knew she was not long for this world. Our parents' and brother's death had told severely upon her strength and it was but too evident she would soon follow them. Sister Minnie did all she could to comfort her; she never wearied nursing the inva-

lid, but watched over her as she had over father
and mother.   She was indeed a devoted daughter and a faithful sister.   Our sister Maria
faded daily; we saw death's signet on her brow;
and as the Reaper "with his sickle keen,"
drew near, she meekly resigned her breath and
fell asleep in the arms of her Saviour.

She bore her sufferings with great fortitude.
We thought our cup of sorrow full to the brim.
Her bereaved husband and his two motherless
children were deeply sympathized with by all
who knew them.   As the stricken father held
his little ones to his heart he felt they were his
only treasures.   They did not know their loss,
their tears were only shed because others older
grown wept.   Very different to me was my
sorrow; I understood how great the void death
made when I was left in the world, a bearer
of one heavy burden, with no mother's watchful care to make it less.   Time had assuaged
the first bitter sense of desolation, my tears
had ceased to fall, but the one star brighter
than all others in my sky had found its way
to another sphere; and from my soul would
come the sad thought;—

"I miss thee, my Mother! Thy image is still
   The deepest impressed on my heart,

And the tablet so faithful, in death must be chill
   Ere a line of that image depart.
Thou wert torn from my side when I treasured thee
     most.
   When my reason could measure thy worth;
When I knew but too well that the idol I'd lose,
   Could be never replaced upon earth.

I miss thee, my Mother, in circles of joy,
   Where I've mingled with rapturous zest;
For how slight is the touch that will serve to destroy
   All the fairy web spun in my breast.
Some melody sweet may be floating around—
   'Tis a ballad I learnt at thy knee;
Some strain may be played, and I shrink from the
     sound,
   For my fingers oft woke it for thee.

I miss thee, my Mother; when health for a season
     has fled,
   And I sink in the languor of pain,
Where, where is the arm that once pillowed my head,
   And the ear that lovingly heard me complain?
Other hands may support, gentle accents may fall—
   For the fond and the true are yet mine:
I've a blessing for each; I am grateful to all—
   But whose care *can* be soothing as thine?

I miss thee, my Mother! Oh, when do I not.
   Though I know 'twas the wisdom of Heaven
That the deepest shade fell on my sunniest spot,
   And such tie of devotion was riven;
For when thou wert with me my soul was below,
   I was chained to the world I then trod;

My affections, my thoughts where all earth-bound;
but now
They have followed thy spirit to God!"

The death of my sister, and the thought of her children being left as they were, so unconscious of what had befallen them, added a keener pang to my heart. I realized afresh the sorrow I had so recently passed through, and I began to think earth was indeed only a vale of tears. Sister Minnie and I took the little motherless ones and endeavored to the utmost of our ability to supply the place of the dear one they had lost. When Mr. I. married again, we transferred our charge to the care of his wife. She very soon succeeded in winning their love as she strove to do her whole duty to those Providence had entrusted to her.

The threads of my simple, quiet life are gathered together. The recital has not been very startling, I am well aware, yet doubtless there has been outlined the prototype of more lives than any herein wrought out; for not many are great or wise in this world of ours. The humbler walks of life are the crowded ways. The few alone scale Alpine heights, or move in solitary grandeur through the throng.

A few closing points may not weary our very patient reader, and I will give them 'ere I say adieu. Sister Minnie and I connected ourselves with the Third Reformed Church, the one in which I had been confirmed some years before, and of which I had been a member during my association with the Institution. We found the congregation as I had known it formerly, composed of generous-hearted, sympathetic people, always willing to do good to any among them they found less blessed by Providence than themselves. Rev. Dr. Gans had succeeded the former pastor. He had gained the affection of his flock; and like a good shepherd he entreated them tenderly and earnestly to feed in religion's pastures and green fields, that their souls might grow in good works, ripening for the kingdom on high. Dr. G. is a pious and saintly man, and his influence can only advance the cause for which he toils.

Mr. John Rodenmayer has a large class of young ladies in the Sabbath School; and I have for some time enjoyed his instruction and christian counsel, and have greatly profited thereby. The school has an able Superintendent in Mr. Wm. F. Richstein.

When we had been awhile settled in Baltimore, we were greatly distressed to learn the death of a dear friend, formerly a resident of Middletown, but who latterly had made the West her home, Miss Clara Williamson. She was young and beautiful and life was full of promise for her, but the Destroyer came and the roses paled before the lilies' breath. She was generally beloved and many eulogies were paid her memory. So pretty, so gentle and sweet,—

"'Tis difficult to feel that she is dead,
  Her presence like the shadow of a wing
  That is just lessening in the upper sky,
  Lingers upon us. We can hear her voice
  And for her step we listen—and the eye
  Looks for her wonted coming—with a strange
  Forgetful earnestness.

Many others who were our kind sympathizers when distresses followed close upon each other, we shall hold in lasting remembrance. A number were unwearying in their attentions, and though we are now separated still we love to linger upon their many acts of friendship. Such as these are often with us in thought when "the hours of day are numbered," and we sit down to ponder upon the loved and distant ones.   When the chilly Autumn shuts us, at the even time, within doors, memory brings back to us these absent friends, these guests of the heart.   Often I sit musing upon them,— while

"Soft falls through the gathering twilight,
    The rain from the dripping eaves,
And stirs with a tremulous rustle
 . The dead and dying leaves;
While afar, in the midst of the shadows,
    I hear the sweet voices of bells,
Come borne on the wind of the Autumn,
    That fitfully rises and swells.

They call and they answer each other,
    They answer and mingle again,
As the deep and the shrill in an anthem
    Make harmony still in their strain,
As the voices of sentinels mingle
    In the mountainous regions of snow,
Till from hill-top to hill-top a chorus
    Floats down to the valleys below.

The shadows, the firelight of even,
    The sound of the rain's distant chime,
Come bringing, with rain softly dropping,
    Sweet thoughts of a shadowy time;
The slumberous sense of seclusion,
    From storm and intruders aloof,
We feel when we hear in the midnight
    The patter of rain on the roof.

When the spirit goes forth in its yearnings
  To take all its wanderers home;
Or, afar, in the regions of fancy,
  Delights on swift pinions to roam,
I quietly sit by the firelight—
  The firelight so bright and so warm—
For I know those only who love me
  Will seek me through shadow and storm.

But should they be absent this evening,
  Should even the household depart,
Deserted, I should not be lonely,
  There still would be guests in my heart.
The faces of friends that I cherish,
  The smile, and the grasp and the tone,
Will haunt me wherever I wander,
  And thus I am never alone.

With those who have left far behind them
  The joys and the sorrows of time—
Who sing the sweet songs of the angels
  In a purer and holier clime.
Then darkly, O, evening of Autumn,
  Your rain and your shadows may fall:
My loved and my lost ones you bring me—
  My heart holds a feast with them all."

CHAPTER XXIII.

"We live in deeds, not years—in thoughts, not breaths—
In feelings not in figures on a dial;
We should count time by heart-throbs. He most lives,
Who thinks most—feels the noblest—acts the best."
Bailey's Festus.

"Heaven doth with us as we with torches do;
Not light them for themselves; for if our virtues
Did not go forth of us 'twere all alike
As if we had them not."
Shakspere's Measure for Measure.

"Fare the well,—and may th' indulgent gods
*   *   *   *   grant thee every wish
Thy soul can form! Once more farewell!"
Sophocles.

"A double blessing is a double grace;
Occasion smiles upon a second leave.
There,—my blessing with you!"
Shakspere's Hamlet.

The narration of the events of our quite life
is now complete. We hope it has afforded a
degree of pleasure. There remains now but a
parting tribute of gratitude to who have for
many years been the warm friends and eloquent advocates of the cause of the blind, and
who have by their practical benevolence done

much towards lifting this unfortunate class out of darkness into the marvellous light of knowledge.

Among these in honored distinction as the earliest friends who undertook the effort to educate the blind should be named—the late Judge Glenn, Jacob I. Cohen, and Charles Howard; these gentlemen labored zealously and verily their good works have followed them; their earnest endeavors are now historic, but these philantropists, pioneers in the cause, as they were, will be often spoken or gratefully by those who never knew them, yet who still have reaped the benefit of their liberality.

Jacob Trust, Benjamin F. Newcomer and Dr. Wm. Fisher have been at all times devoted to this benevolence, and will ever be warmly appreciated by all in whose behalf they have shown so great interest.

J. Howard McHenry, President of the Board of Directors, and John T. Morris, for a number of years the efficient Secretary, should have high encomium for their labors for the advancement of the blind. They express the humanitarian in their every act, large in sympathy, liberal in the practical development of the same, and with the most enlightened views as to the probable good that may be attained by a careful study of the cause, they justly receive from those they so magnanimously serve, gratitude, that no words may adequately express; but which pulsates in hearts full to overflowing with appreciation of their many deeds of kindness.

If a man or woman wishes to realize the full power of living, it must be by cherishing noble hopes and purposes; by having something to do and something to live for, which is worthy of humanity, and which, by expanding the capacities of the soul, elevates to God-like capabilities the whole being, giving expansion and symmetry as well to the body, which contains the spiritual essence of existence, and beautifying it with dignified expression. This is no new argument but one old as Creation itself. It is besides sound philosophy, and we may indulge a just pride that among our fellow men are to be found exponents every day and every where of this elevated teaching. There are those all around us whose first aim in life is to aid the needy, to lift the fallen, to cheer the bereaved; and there are no holier offices, no more pious purposes.

We have alluded gratefully, as we found it in our heart to do, to the Officers and Directors of the Institution for the instruction of the blind, Maryland's greatest benevolence; and we must not in this connection omit reference to the Committee of Female Visitors. Many of these ladies have been friends of the Institution during its years of trial and vicissitude, have taken active interest in this noble charity, and have at last, as a result of the harmonious working of all who had espoused it, the satisfaction of seeing their labors crowned with success. Among these kind patrons, while all are thankfully remembered, we may be permitted to make especial mention of Mrs. Isabella Brown; this lady has been a large contributor to the material prosperity and general welfare of the blind. We have thus far made no mention of the friend and physician of the Institution, Dr. James A. Steuart; but we are not willing to close the book without testifying to his watchfulness and care. The general health of the pupils was largely attributable to his skillful supervision. We appreciated this, for had our every other blessing been continued, and this one not been ours to enjoy, existence in the Institution with all its privileges, would have been only a weariness.

Now Gentle Reader, a tender wish, a loving word, a fond adieu, and we part, myself the happier that we have met; for your perusal of the pages of the modest life presented you, has encouraged, though so silently, the endeavor made to draw some teachings from usual experiences, and make them interesting.

We hope no shadow, that can not be removed, has darkened your path; but that the light of Nature's glorious Sun has shone upon your outward life, as that of the Sun of Righteousness has illumed your inner being, making bright with happiness that cannot pale or change, all your soul's fair chambers.

For ourselves we have learned the blissful truth of Jehovah's promise,—" I will bring the blind by a way that they knew not; I will lead them in paths that they have not known: I will make darkness light before them, and crooked things straight. These things will I do unto them and not forsake them." He has said, and His word cannot fail, He would "open the blind eyes," this to us is a precious thought, which though in its fullest sense we may not realize with our earthly vision, yet in the Great Beyond we know that we shall with rapturous exhultation,

> "Hail, holy Light, offspring of Heav'n first-born,
> Or of th' Eternal co-eternal beam,
> Bright effluence of bright essence increate."

Our spirits take fresh courage in the blest assurance, and look upon this lower life as but the vestibule of that higher one we hope to attain.

The story is told unto its end, and yet we linger to leave a last adieu for the kindly scanner of these pages. We shall never meet again, but we are friends, and shall ever think gently of each other;—a moment, and we are separated:

> "I have no parting glance to give,
> So take my parting smile."

www.ingramcontent.com/pod-product-compliance
Lightning Source LLC
Chambersburg PA
CBHW030124030726
47498CB00007B/2542